THE BORN SURVIVOR

THE BORN SURVIVOR

Lauran Paine

CHIVERS

THORNDIKE

LgPt Pai

This Large Print book is published by BBC Audiobooks Ltd, Bath, England and by Thorndike Press®, Waterville, Maine, USA.

Published in 2005 in the U.K. by arrangement with Golden West Literary Agency

Published in 2005 in the U.S. by arrangement with Golden West Literary Agency

U.K. Hardcover ISBN 1–4056–3282–8 (Chivers Large Print)
U.S. Softcover   ISBN 0–7862–7464–6 (Nightingale)

The text of this Large Print edition is unabridged.
Other aspects of the book may vary from the original edition.

Set in 16 pt. New Times Roman.

Printed in Great Britain on acid-free paper.

British Library Cataloguing in Publication Data available

Library of Congress Cataloging-in-Publication Data

Paine, Lauran.
       The born survivor / by Lauran Paine.
            p.   cm. — (Thorndike Press large print Nightingale)
       ISBN 0–7862–7464–6 (lg. print : sc : alk. paper)
       1. Private investigators—California—Los Angeles—Fiction.
       2. Married women—Crimes against—Fiction. 3. Turks—United
       States—Fiction. 4. Los Angeles (Calif.)—Fiction. 5. Large type
       books. I. Title. II. Series.
       PS3566.A34B68 2005
       813'.54—dc22   2004030756

Chapter One

James A. Garfield was the twentieth president of the United States. He died at the hand of an assassin in the year 1881. He was no Great Emancipator, no advocate of Manifest Destiny, and too late to be the Father of his Country. In fact, he was not an especially colourful president at all, and for that reason, while there have always been sons given the names George Washington, Abraham Lincoln, Ulysses Grant, and even Edward Kennedy, there had not been many given the surnames of James Garfield. Even if they had been given that name, not too many people would recall that there had been a US President named James Garfield.

Also, one might reasonably wonder why anyone would want to name a son after a president whose memory was as lacklustre as was that of President Garfield—except for his alleged acceptance of a bribe, and even that wasn't very earth-shaking, because the sum was $329. Not enough by current standards, to make the down-payment on much of a car. Even in his scandals, then, James Adam Garfield was not particularly notorious nor outstanding.

Nor was James Garfield Hewlett able to explain why he had been named after the president, beyond saying that his grandfather had served under President Garfield in some minor capacity, which really wasn't much of an explanation; his *father* had served under another US president, Franklin Roosevelt, and there were quite a few sons around surnamed Franklin Roosevelt, so, presumably, that would have been a better likelihood, except that it hadn't obtained, so Jim Hewlett had been named after that other president, and in any event, it wasn't something that cropped up in conversation very often; a president who had gone to his reward almost a century earlier scarcely ever achieved even casual mention, outside the stultified halls of academe, and even there he didn't make the scene very often.

Jim Hewlett's acceptance of the name had inevitably been philosophical; after all, a person couldn't very well rebel against something as shadowy as the origin of his name, even if he was the kind of a person who rebelled, which Jim Hewlett was not.

He'd never had to rebel. Aside from having been born into a moderately well-off family, having attended good schools, having been an affable, rather ruggedly handsome individual, Jim Hewlett had also matured at an inch over six feet, and had stopped gaining weight at slightly over two hundred pounds. That kind of man did not have to rebel very often.

The nearest he had come to it, after

achieving manhood, had been when his family had learned that Jim Hewlett had become licensed in the city of Los Angeles, California, as a private investigator. What, his family had collectively asked, what in the name of God was he *thinking* of? At least, if you *must* become involved on the seamy side, get into proper, municipal, police work, but a private investigator . . . ! That was someone who spied on erring wives, who hired out as some politician's bodyguard, and those were the *good* jobs.

Jim Hewlett had been smiling his way through differences of opinion since he'd been twenty years old, and had reached his optimum height and weight. Before that, he'd occasionally had to support opinions physically. After that, those extremely rare occasions when he still had to support them physically, found Jim Hewlett, the former inter-collegiate boxer and wrestler, entirely capable. But his smile was usually adequate— that, and what was very obviously behind it.

Jim hadn't argued with his family, and as someone had once noted about Jim Hewlett, how *did* you successfully employ diamond-hard and crystal-clear logic, against an adversary who was big enough to go bear hunting with a flyswatter, and who simply exuded good nature and charm, and instead of opposing you in argument, simply slapped you on the back and smiled, while you were talking yourself blue in the face?

The family's chagrin was masked, on those rare occasions, such as Christmas or someone's birthday, when Jim showed up to join the tribe. Otherwise, very little mention was made of either Jim or his vocation.

Families drifted apart; that was the age-old sequence. Girls got married and became engrossed with their own families. Boys got married, too, but their interests became even more diversified, between families, and business, and sometimes hobbies like golf or tennis, or other girls, but whatever the vocation or avocation, part of the process of maturity was drifting apart.

Jim Hewlett had been drifting apart since his first couple of years at the University; perhaps he'd been drifting apart from the rest of the family even before that; certainly his interests had not coincided with theirs, even earlier. His father was in banking; not *high* in banking, but secure in it. One of his sisters had married a man who belonged to the Department of Transportation, which was one of those completely fatuous, quite dispensible dumping-grounds for people who had achieved college degrees without any heritage of intelligence. His sister's husband could not actually have succeeded as a plumber or as an electrician, let alone a carpenter, but his college degree had made him eligible for the Department of Transportation, and he enjoyed the exclusive distinction of all people lacking intelligence who achieved college degrees—he could prove to you just how much of a complete sub-mediocrity he was, through the use of good English.

His other sister had married a man who was also in banking, a nice, weak, pliable individual who had a delightful personality and the willpower of a jellyfish. But for this particular sister no other kind of a mate would have sufficed; she was, like Jim Hewlett's mother, strong-willed, opinionated, and domineering.

Jim Hewlett was the alien. In a family of noteworthy conformists and mediocrities, he was the non-conformist, the individual of bullet-like perception, fast reactions, and a very unique degree of tolerance. He was also shrewd, and of course, selective; a man like Jim Hewlett never would have broken out of the mould unless he had been selective.

His first four assignments had been surveillances for divorce lawyers. He had only undertaken one of them; the other three he had respectfully declined. Selectivity led Jim Hewlett to postpone a few meals, but he good-naturedly, and stubbornly, declined to compromise with it, so, for the first three years of his vocational launching, he did not prosper. In fact he hardly ate. But the few cases he did accept for lawyers, which were not in any way connected with someone trying to catch a spouse bed-hopping, he handled expertly. In fact, by the close of the third year, no one referred divorce cases to him, but several law firms engaged him for other types of investigations, and by the middle of his fourth year, he was officially launched by locating and bringing into the open, handcuffed, incidentally, the daughter of a wealthy and prominent San Francisco family, who was emotionally about six years of age, and intellectually about nine years of age, who had joined a terrorist group, for the same reason others from less notable families had also belonged to the same group—incurable, lifelong, immaturity.

Jim Hewlett never disclosed how he had managed to accomplish this feat, which the police had failed at. He even declined an offer of fifty thousand dollars from a newspaper syndicate for the story—and that also made news. The number of people, but especially private investigators, who turned down fifty thousand dollars for simply writing the story of their most successful coup, was very minute.

But between the successful conclusion of this particular assignment, and his refusal to capitalise on it, upon the grounds that to do so would violate a confidence, Jim Hewlett became an almost overnight success.

He rented an office in West Los Angeles, which was *the* place to have offices. He hired a girl named Mary Friday—whom he called simply 'Friday'—as his secretary, and he moved from a walk-up flat to a delightful ground floor apartment on the fringe of Beverly Hills, which had, among other conveniences, a secluded, walled-in, beautifully landscaped, patio.

And he began to feel a little breathless each time the first of the month rolled round. But he always had the money to meet his obligations, along with a bit left over. By the end of his fourth year, there was quite a bit left over. For the first time in his life he had a bank account. Also, for the first time in his life, he had that deep-down sense of satisfaction a man can only possess when he has met the world on its own terms, and compelled it to pay him well for his personal talents. It was a feeling fewer and fewer human beings enjoyed, and presumably, even that small number would predictably diminish rather steadily as the Race of Man continued to breed up the quantity of its members, and not the quality of them.

There was always the Department of Transportation, though.

Jim Hewlett had some aversions. They arose from business contacts with clients based in specific industries. He did not encourage clients who were connected with the motion picture industry, or in general, the entertainment industry. He avoided implication with racketeers of any kind, those under the unsmiling eye of the police, or those

7

at places like City Hall who hid their deceitfulness and dishonesty with, usually, total success.

This did, in fact, limit his clientele, but Jim Hewlett had as his source of employment what was probably the largest professional group of people in all of California—the lawyers.

Those were the people he cultivated, and they, in turn, were the people who either employed him outright or referred the majority of his clients to him. The day when counsellors at law had done their own leg-work, had long passed. Sophisticated, knowledgeable private investigators such as James Garfield Hewlett did it for them, and of course for a fee, which in turn invariably came from the percentages the law firms got from their clients, for successful prosecutions which normally ended in stiff judgements.

It was, as Mary Friday told Jim Hewlett after a particularly large cheque had been received, the cleanest way she knew, for a person to become wealthy from a dirty business.

His response had been to charm her with his rugged good looks, his warmly disarming smile, and a superb dinner at a very exclusive supper club, complete with very old wine, and a promise of undying love instead of a raise.

It was very hard even momentarily to stand in opposition to a man like that. Mary knew it, Jim'Hewlett knew it, and quite a number of other people, but especially women, had certainly come to know it. The trouble was, that behind the extravagant charm was something with the hardness of cold-rolled steel, and *that* was the part of Jim Hewlett very few people, but *especially* women, understood at all.

Chapter Two

The city of Los Angeles would have made an enviable independent democracy, or monarchy, or autocracy. It was practically self-sufficient; more self-sufficient at any rate, than were almost any of the civilised nations. It had within its ever-expanding boundaries some of the most efficient farming enclaves on earth. It also had a wealth-producing base greater than any in the Soviet Union or the People's Republic of China. It had more people than many nations twice or three times its size, and it possessed one of the fast-growing, skilled, populations in the world.

If that wasn't enough, it also had the law firm of Benedict and Fleisher, rated among the finest legal consortiums in the US, with overseas affiliates—amply subsidised of course—in such diverse places as London, Bombay, Tokyo and Casablanca. The Benedict and Fleisher clientele was not extensive, and never had been, but it *was* very influential, very cosmopolitan, and very rich, things which compensated for quantity, or, as the junior partner named Carl Hollingsworth, explained to Jim Hewlett the day he kept an appointment in Hewlett's private office, Benedict and Fleisher only handled assignments which could be given their fullest attention, and their very best efforts, and for that reason the clients of Benedict and Fleisher who would be so served by this dean of legal establishments, were kept nameless when Benedict and Fleisher found it expedient to bring in outside corollaries, in this instance, the private investigative services of James G. Hewlett, who had come most highly recommended for his discretion, his tasteful expertise, and his record of successful achievements.

Jim Hewlett sat through all this with his hooded, but smiling, blue eyes, unwaveringly upon the immaculate man across the desk from him, making a total assessment of Carl Hollingsworth, and when it had been indirectly explained what the ground rules would be, although Jim was impressed, not by what had been said about him, but at having been chosen to do anything at all for Benedict and Fleisher, he said, 'I appreciate the standards of Benedict and Fleisher. What, exactly, is it that you have in mind?' meaning that he would reserve judgement upon whether he would work according to the Benedict and Fleisher ground rules.

Hollingsworth smiled faintly, as though to imply a cameraderie which *might*, just *might*, come out of this private discussion. Then he said, 'Mr Benedict has instructed me to refer to our client only as Astarte. You'll be familiar with mythology. It's a mythological

11

symbiosis—sort of.'

Jim Hewlett smiled and murmured, 'That's nice.'

'Astarte, Mr Hewlett, has been a victim of embezzlement. Benedict and Fleisher have been engaged to pursue a course based upon restitution. In full, you understand.'

Hewlett sighed. 'Mr Hollingsworth, embezzlement is a felony. The police will be happy to—'

'Mr Hewlett, you needn't explain the functions of the police to me,' stated Hollingsworth, still faintly smiling. 'I didn't make my point, then did I? This entire matter is to be affected *without* the police.'

Jim Hewlett brought his chair forward, leaned both thick arms upon the desktop, and stared steadily at his visitor. 'You don't need me to explain the functions of the police to you. All right, I won't do it. And I'm going to assume, Mr Hollingsworth, that you know damned well that withholding information relative to the commission of a felony—is a misdemeanour. So, what you're hinting, is that I do something outside the law for the law firm of—'

'Absolutely not,' stated Hollingsworth, breaking in sharply. 'This embezzlement did not occur in the United States.'

Jim Hewlett continued to lean on the desk gazing steadily at his visitor. 'I see. It didn't happen in the US. And where *did* it happen, and wherever that is, are you implying that they don't have any equivalent laws concerning embezzlement, and the withholding of information?'

Carl Hollingsworth's faint smile dwindled. He smoothed his jacket and adjusted his tie. He gazed a little stonily at Jim Hewlett, then he answered. 'Astarte is not a US citizen. I'm sure you're aware that Benedict and Fleisher are internationally connected. This particular embezzlement was committed in Turkey—well—it was committed on the ocean, within Turkish jurisdictional waters, you see. But—and of course Turkish law defines embezzlement as our equivalent to a felony—but, you must understand this: the embezzlement was committed by a man against his wife, and according to my research, Turkish views on community property, and our laws on that subject, are not very compatible. So—Astarte is here, in Los Angeles—in the US—as a client of Benedict and Fleisher, and we have engaged to attempt a full restitution. Which is where you come in. Now, have I made the matter clearer?'

Jim Hewlett, still leaning on the desk staring at Carl Hollingsworth, barely inclined his head. 'Clearer,' he mumbled, echoing Hollingsworth. 'Why don't Benedict and Fleisher just simply institute action against the husband—a civil rather than a criminal, action—and get the money or bonds, or whatever it is that he took, handed back?'

'Because, Mr Hewlett, and I'm surprised you overlooked this, the crime was not committed within the territorial limits of the United States. Also, there's another reason why we can't bring legal suit in a US court: the husband is in Turkey.'

Hewlett leaned back. 'You are suggesting, then, that I go to Turkey, try to twist this guy's arm, get the bonds or whatever it is, and fly home with them—for Astarte?'

'For Benedict and Fleisher, Mr Hewlett. You will not at any time make an effort to contact Astarte. That's to be part of the agreement. Incidentally, I have an original copy of a legal and binding agreement with me.' Hollingsworth reached inside his jacket.

Jim Hewlett shook his head. 'Never mind the agreement, just answer the question. You want me to fly to Turkey and—?'

'No. That won't be necessary. The man will be arriving in Canada as part of a Turkish trade commission within ten days. You can intercept him there.'

'And you expect him to come with a trade commission, carrying the bonds in his pocket?'

Carl Hollingsworth smiled. 'Benedict and Fleisher have very good sources of information. We expect the man to arrive in Canada, *with* either the bonds or their cash equivalent, because he has been known to say that he will not invest in Turkey, or any of the other troubled nations of his part of the world. So you see, he *will* have the embezzled collateral or its equivalent.' Hollingworth's smile widened. 'He is masking his real purpose in leaving Turkey and coming to the Western Hemisphere, with this trade commission, you see. His real purpose is to put his wealth where it will not only be safe, but where it will yield him interest and dividends which he couldn't hope for in Turkey.'

'How much, exactly, are we talking about, Mr Hollingsworth? The reason I ask, is because my fee is not small.'

'We are talking about a hundred million dollars, Mr Hewlett. Its US equivalent, you'll understand.'

Jim Hewlett nodded. 'Naturally—its US equivalent.' He let his breath out soundlessly, and sucked back a big, fresh lungful. 'A hundred million dollars. Is this in bonds?'

'Well, when it was embezzled it was all in bonds, yes, but that was last month, and since that time it may have been converted to currency, or to other bonds. We can't really be certain. Understandably, the man is very wary.'

'He can't be *too* wary, Mr Hollingsworth, if he's willing to come to the Western Hemisphere, knowing his—knowing that Astarte is here, and perhaps also knowing that she has engaged Benedict and Fleisher.'

'He thinks she is dead, Mr Hewlett. You see, he stabbed her, and threw the body into the sea, which is how he managed to bring the thing off so well with the Turkish authorities, who consider him her legal heir.'

Hewlett gave that little nod again. 'Stabbed her and threw her into the sea . . . Mr Hollingsworth, what, exactly, does this man do for a living—I mean, besides kill his wives for their wealth?'

'He has been a member of a militant Turkish opium-exporting concern . . . I'll be honest with you: He has been in charge of eliminating foreign spies or whatever you care to call them, who have been keeping an eye on Turkish opium farmers, among the Western nations which oppose Turkish opium farming.'

Jim Hewlett's broad brow got two deep creases across it, as he sat staring at Hollingsworth. He said, 'Let's just knock this down to the basics, Mr Hollingsworth. You—all right, Benedict and Fleisher, then—want to hire me to convince a Turkish assassin that he should hand over a hundred million dollars he took from a woman he thought he'd murdered, and you want me to do this in another country, and you know damned well there is no way I can do it without violating the laws of Canada, and if I'm caught and charged in Canada—'

'Benedict and Fleisher will represent you, Mr Hewlett.'

'Oh. That makes it all right, doesn't it? Are you aware what kind of an international

16

incident could come out of this, if I'm unsuccessful, or if I'm caught?'

'But that's exactly why Benedict and Fleisher want you, and not someone else, to undertake the assignment, Mr Hewlett. You will not be caught.' Hollingsworth's smile lingered around his small, fat lips. 'It's getting late in the day, and we haven't discussed the matter of your fee, have we?'

Jim Hewlett said, 'I don't think we're going to discuss it.'

'One hundred thousand dollars, and all expenses, Mr Hewlett.'

In four years, including the current year, his best one to date, Jim Hewlett had not totalled quite half that much money.

Carl Hollingsworth, studying the larger, thicker man across the desk from him, slowly reached into his jacket and brought forth two envelopes, one crisply white with Benedict and Fleisher's suite address in the city engraved upon it, the other envelope larger, bulkier, and manila-brown.

Hollingsworth arose, placed both envelopes in front of Jim Hewlett, glanced at a solid gold wristwatch, and gave a small sigh of resignation. 'I do wish I had more time, Mr Hewlett. I have to make an appearance in court this afternoon in an estate hearing.' His eyes came up slowly. 'I'll leave all the particulars, and the agreement requiring your notarised signature, with you. Perhaps you

17

could call me in the morning. My card's also enclosed.'

Jim Hewlett watched Hollingsworth depart without saying a word. After the door had been discreetly closed, he reached for his intercom, punched a button and said, 'Friday—who the hell is Astarte?'

The brown-eyed girl with the peaches-and-cream complexion in the outer office answered matter-of-factly. 'Not *is,* Mr Hewlett, *was.* Astarte was a goddess of the Phoenicians and Assyrians. The Chaldean called her Ishtar, and I think the Babylonians called her Nana. Anything else?'

'Yes; why do you always manage to put me down?'

The softly matter-of-fact voice answered with just a faint hint of amusement in it, 'I don't. Well, I don't *deliberately* do it. You just happened to hit the jackpot that time. Mythology is my thing. I'd rather read mythology than Sartre. It's all there, Mr Hewlett, all the romance, violence, politics. I'll loan you a very good book on it if you'd like me to. There is nothing that has happened in our world which didn't happen many times in *their* world. About that book . . .'

Jim Hewlett said, 'No thank you. Maybe another time,' and switched off the intercom to open the first envelope, the one with the Benedict and Fleisher address in the upper left hand corner.

The agreement was three pages long, double-spaced, and as incisive as it could be, while at the same time being all-inclusive. But it never once mentioned the nature of the undertaking it represented; it simply bound James G. Hewlett to observe absolute secrecy with respect of any assignment he might ever undertake for the law firm of Benedict and Fleisher, along with a whole host of other inhibitory enjoinders which, if Jim Hewlett signed it, would bind him to Benedict and Fleisher as thoroughly as though it were being done with steel chains.

The only thing he did not resent was the shortest, and last paragraph. There, it was set forth that he was to be reimbursed in the amount of one hundred thousand dollars, and all expenses, for undertaking this assignment, such sums not to be in any way contingent upon success or failure.

That meant, whether he found the Turk and got the whatever-it-was back, for the client called Astarte, he would be paid one hundred thousand dollars—and expenses.

He carefully placed this unique document aside, and reached for the bulky manila envelope. His secretary called to say it was five o'clock, and she was leaving for the day, before Jim Hewlett was aware that so much time had passed since Carl Hollingsworth had first entered his office.

Chapter Three

The Turk's name was Hamid Rumi. There was a small photograph of him, about the size of a passport picture, showing a man with rather pleasant features, large, dark eyes, and an almost kindly expression.

Whatever Jim Hewlett had expected, this was not it. He studied the photograph for a long time, then laid it aside to read what Benedict and Fleisher had dug up on his background. The information was rather extensive, indicating that Benedict and Fleisher had a good source, and that was interesting too.

Finally, he read what had been produced on the attempted murder of Hamid Rumi's wife, and here, at least, there was much less authentic information. In fact, it was limited to the bare fact that the woman had been stabbed and hurled into the sea from a luxury liner travelling between Crete and the Turkish mainland. The report did not even mention Hamid Rumi. His name only appeared later, in the woman's account of the physical attack, and as Jim Hewlett read this, slowly, an idea began to firm up in his mind that perhaps Hamid Rumi had not attacked the woman at all. For one thing, the attack occurred on deck, well after dinner, when it was dark. For another thing, she was stabbed in the back, indicating that she'd had no warning, and finally when she was found and pulled from the sea by a small fishing boat, while the fisherman was doing his utmost to save her life, she opened her eyes, accused him of attempting to murder her, and would have fought him if she'd been able.

The evidence that her husband *had* committed the attempted murder lay in the fact that as soon as the liner docked, he reported her dead, and filed for possession of her estate.

There was one question the Benedict and Fleisher report neglected to mention. How had the woman, Astarte, happened to have such vast wealth? There were other questions Jim Hewlett would have liked the answers to, but as he carefully put all the papers back into their envelopes, and arose to leave the office, he had no sense of urgency; it said in the report that the Turkish trade commission would not be arriving in Canada for another ten days, which was also what Hollingsworth had told him. He could fly to Canada in a matter of hours, could arrive there the day before, and still have plenty of time.

At home, he went back over the papers, then poured himself a stiff Scotch and soda, stepped out upon the flagstones of his patio and gazed up where the moon was making its majestic crossing.

If he signed the Benedict and Fleisher agreement, which was actually, in legal terminology, a contract rather than an agreement, he would be launching himself into something he really did not feel entirely qualified for. Up until now, his cases hadn't had the least bit of international flavour to them, and also, up until now he had not stretched nor bent any laws, and regardless of Hollingsworth's double-talk, this time he would have to bend some laws, would probably have to break some, in fact.

As for the fee, it was practically unheard of, at his level of private investigating. But there were two things which interested him. One, was the possibility that Hamid Rumi actually had not tried to kill his wife, and in filing for her estate had acted normally—maybe a little hastily, but normally. The other thing was the fact that she was a woman. Jim Hewlett had some notion that you *pushed* girls, you didn't *strike* them, and certainly not with a knife in your hand.

Then of course there was something else: If it turned out that Hamid Rumi had *not* tried to kill his wife, that someone else, for whatever reason, had done that, and Jim Hewlett could come up with conclusive proof to this effect, he would not have to bend any Canadian laws, he would have a pleasant sojourn up north— and he would still be eligible to collect the hundred thousand dollars, plus expenses.

He drained the glass, returned to the sunken living-room, rummaged for a pen and signed the agreement, shoved it back into its envelope, and went off to bed.

He was committed.

In the morning he was already in his office when Mary Friday arrived, and looked in at the door, surprised. She said, 'Good morning. Would you like a cup of coffee?'

He smiled at her, accepted the offer, then, while she was gone, he dialled Benedict and Fleisher and asked for Mr Hollingsworth. When the connection was completed, Hewlett said, 'About the fee; there's nothing in the contract defining payment.'

Hollingsworth's reply was prompt. 'Mr Benedict thought that half in advance, and half, plus the expenses, when the assignment has been completed. How does that sound?'

Hewlett had no objections. 'Then you can drop round and pick up the signed contract today, and leave the cheque.'

'Certainly, I'll be glad to,' Hollingsworth said. 'Were there any questions?'

'Just one. Aside from Astarte, who believes it was her husband who stabbed her in the back and pitched her over the side?'

'It was his knife, Mr Hewlett. Isn't that in the report?'

There was no mention of a knife anywhere in the report. 'No, it's not in the report, and how did you know it?'

23

Hollingsworth cleared his throat. 'I'm terribly sorry. The police report from Antora, which was supposed to have been included in the documents. I gave you, is lying right here on my desk. I guess, in my hurry yesterday, I overlooked it. I'll bring it right over.'

Hewlett put down the telephone with a scowl. Benedict and Fleisher didn't make mistakes like that.

Friday came with the coffee, put it in front of him, and smiled directly down into his eyes. 'Problems,' she asked softly, 'so early in the morning?'

He reached for the cup, neglecting to look at her. 'I'm beginning to get a bad feeling. Do you ever do that?'

She nodded. 'Every now and then. Anything I can help with?'

He lifted the cup, looked up, and was held momentarily motionless by her freshness and her beauty. It had happened before. He tasted the coffee before saying, 'I've got to go to Canada.'

The liquid dark eyes continued to regard him warmly. 'That's an improvement over the trip our last client thought you ought to take.'

He sipped more coffee, then put the cup down. His last client had been a loud, overbearing industrialist, and when Hewlett had declined to accept his fee, the industrialist had become abusive. He smiled at Friday. 'You're very clever for so early in the morning.'

He continued to gaze at her. 'How would you like to go along?'

The liquid dark eyes, so deceptively doe-like, did not even waver as she said, 'You've never needed a secretary on trips before. That *is* what you had in mind, isn't it, Mr Hewlett— a secretary?'

He reached for the cup, drained it, and shoved it back across the desk towards her. 'What else would I have in mind?'

She did not answer as she picked up the cup and went to the door, but, from over there, she looked back with a smile, and said, 'I hope you won't be gone long, I'll miss you.' Then she went out and closed the door.

He hardly heard what she'd said. He paced over to the window and gazed down into the busy street, stories below. The bad feeling was nothing substantial, but in its embryonic way, it was there, and he was conscious of it. Private investigators became accustomed to being used. Clients, even the most sincere ones, seldom were totally frank or totally truthful. The feeling he had now, was that Benedict and Fleisher were being that way. Not entirely frank.

For a hundred million dollars, perhaps even Benedict and Fleisher would yield a point or two in ethics, which would normally be all right with Jim Hewlett, but not this time, not if he was going to be jockeyed into a position where he was used in some kind of deadly game among the high-rollers. A hundred thousand dollar fee wasn't worth a plugged penny if no one was around to collect it or spend it.

He went back, delved into the brown envelope for the three-page report again, took it back to the window with him, and carefully re-read what was said there, about Hamid Rumi's background.

The Turk had, for a fact, been an official of a militant protective association connected with Turkey's opium farmers, exactly as Carl Hollingsworth had said, and there was no way to turn anything like that into something altruistic nor benign. Also, he had been an officer in the Turkish army, another organisation not normally suspected of compassionate sympathies. But there was nothing to indicate that Hamid Rumi actually performed assassinations, or perhaps Jim Hewlett was trying to read something into the man's background, which simply did not exist. He studied the passport-size photo again, shook his head, and was returning to the desk when Carl Hollingsworth arrived, smiling, immaculately attired as usual, and perfectly poised.

He greeted Hewlett and handed him an envelope. 'I apologise again, Mr Hewlett. An oversight like this simply proves that mistakes will occur when a man has more work than he can effectively handle.'

Jim took the police report round behind the

desk, motioned Hollingsworth to the chair opposite him, asked if Hollingsworth would care for coffee, and when the offer was politely declined, Jim sat back and read the report.

The weapon used in the attempted homicide had been identified by the Turkish police as having belonged to Hamid Rumi. There was something else; Hamid Rumi had been married once before, to a French woman. She too had died at sea, but her body had only been recovered after several months, along the coast between Nice and Monaco, in the backwater of a small fishing village, and it had been in the water too long for an accurate decision regarding the cause of death to be determined.

There was no mention of the details of that death, and nothing was said in the report of any possible advantages which might have accrued to Hamid Rumi as a result of it.

Hollingsworth shifted slightly in his chair, and discreetly glanced at his watch. Jim saw this and ignored it until he had finished the Turkish police report. As he laid the paper atop the desk he said, 'I'll tell you what I think I'm going to do, Mr Hollingsworth. I think I'm going to spend a couple of days doing my own research on this assignment—before I hand you the signed agreement. Is that acceptable to Benedict and Fleisher?'

Hollingsworth's smooth face reddened just noticeably. 'You're not leaving me much alternative to the feeling that you don't quite trust us,' he said, and Jim Hewlett smiled.

'I'm not sure who it is I don't quite trust,' he told the lawyer. 'And I'm not even quite sure *why* I feel this way.' He continued to smile. 'You're entirely free to find another investigator, Mr Hollingsworth.'

'Mr Benedict has his heart set on you taking the case, Mr Hewlett. I wouldn't want to be the one to disappoint Mr Benedict.'

Jim arose. 'When did you say this Turkish trade commission will arrive in Canada? A little more than a week, wasn't it?'

'Yes.'

'Well, we have plenty of time then, it seems to me.' Hewlett went to the door and laid a hand lightly upon the knob, smiling at the man who was reluctantly coming up to his feet across the room and moving towards the door, 'A day or two won't matter. It might even help a little.' He opened the door and still held the knob in his hand, blocking the opening with his body. 'Mr Hollingsworth, if I go to Canada I'll need something a lot more definite than I've got about those securities, or whatever, Rumi is bringing with him. I can't just brace the man and demand that he make restitution, because the moment I walk away, he *and* the loot, is going to disappear.'

Hollingsworth flopped his arms. 'I don't know what to tell you. We don't know what'll he turn up with, cash or bonds, or maybe even something tangible like gold or jewels. The

bonds he embezzled were negotiable anywhere in the world. He could have turned
them into cash, bought diamonds or—'

'How the hell do you make embezzlement out
of a clear case of inheritance, Mr Hollingsworth?
Even the Turkish police couldn't nail Rumi,
and that's where it happened.'

'I make it embezzlement, Mr Hewlett, for
the simple reason that he could not inherit,
under Turkish law or our law, while his wife
was alive, which she is.'

'Then why doesn't she notify the Turkish
consulate here, and get some kind of
restraining order prohibiting him from—?'

'Because she is mortally afraid that if he
finds out he didn't kill her, he'll do a better job
of it next time—right here in Los Angeles. Mr
Hewlett, you've got to understand by now, that
regardless of your scepticism, this man is very,
very dangerous. The moment she appears at
the Turkish consulate, and the fact that she
isn't dead reaches Turkey, Rumi will most
certainly try again. After all, we're talking
about a hundred million dollars.'

Jim Hewlett let the dispute rest there. He
moved aside for Hollingsworth to depart, and
they exchanged a chilly nod. Hewlett stood in
the doorway, watching, until Hollingsworth
vanished beyond the outer door, then he
caught Mary Friday eyeing him, and turned
back into his private office, closing the door
after himself.

29 DISCARD

Chapter Four

The sources for information about Turkish soldiers, assassins, or even Turkish trade commissioners who were accredited to Canada, were not so readily available in the United States that picking up a telephone created the effect of an Open Sesame.

He knew no one at the Turkish consulate, and even if he had, he would have been putting everything in jeopardy by calling them.

The newspapers were ordinarily a superb source of information about famous, or infamous, people—but the number of Turks in the United States had to be very small, and to Jim Hewlett's knowledge, aside from one mediocre Turkish actor some years back, during Hewlett's youth, he couldn't recall a single Turkish luminary who had made the newspapers, either as a resident, or as a visitor to the country.

He had one contact, a man named Clarence Bryson of the local FBI office, with whom Hewlett had co-operated several times over the past four years, who just might be able to help.

Not because the FBI would have anything on a Turk whose background did not intimate that he had ever even visited the US. The FBI was limited to internal, national, security. But

Bryson had a number of excellent contacts in another federal agency which could, conceivably, have something on a Turk who had been involved in the opium traffic—the Central Intelligence Agency.

Hewlett called Bryson, told him what he wanted, told him as much as Bryson had to know about why Hewlett was interested, and was relieved when Clarence Bryson promised to do the requisite spade work and call back, later in the day, or, if it was after working hours, Bryson said he would contact Hewlett at home.

That was an immense relief for Jim Hewlett. Even though it was entirely feasible that the CIA would have nothing on Hamid Rumi.

Ordinarily, Jim Hewlett would not have let the matter rest there, but today he did. He told Mary Friday he was going home for the day, when it was barely one o'clock in the afternoon, and departed under her mildly reproachful, and wondering, liquid soft gaze.

The weather was hot, but that hardly discouraged a man from working who had grown up in Southern California. It may have been the magnitude of this assignment, its complications as well as its implications, which made Jim Hewlett restless. It may also have been the knowledge that all he'd had to do that morning to receive a cheque for fifty thousand dollars, was hand over the signed contract to Carl Hollingsworth, and he hadn't done it.

Jim wasn't sure, himself, what made him want to get away from the office for the balance of the day, but as soon as he drove down to the Santa Monica breakwater where he kept his twenty-four-foot auxiliary sailboat, and went out in the tethered dinghy, he at least knew what he *needed*; this particular kind of therapy. He had been sailing the coastal waters since he'd been a youngster, but until he'd bought the sailboat last year, and had spent a lot of time overhauling it, last winter, he'd never owned a craft of his own.

He ducked down into the tiny cabin, changed into dungarees, sneakers, and a battered old floppy cotton hat, then climbed back on deck, his upper body, which was already tanned, exposed to the dazzling sunlight which bounced upwards from the blue-green sea.

Today, he did not winch up the anchor. Today, he was completely satisfied simply to loll on the forward deck with the lift and gentle lurch of the boat lulling him into a wonderful torpor. He lay face-down, chin resting on one big fist, gazing back in the direction of the shore, sorting through the details, as many of them as he knew at the present time, of the Astarte affair.

He did not even know he'd fallen asleep until the gentle warping of his boat, a rhythmic motion of pleasant little lifts and rolls, was broken, after so many hours, by the abrupt lurching of the deck to starboard. It was the break in the rhythm that awakened him. He didn't even hear his name until it had been said several times, then he raised up and turned, blinking both eyes against the lingering brilliance of sunlight off water.

His visitor was not dusky, although her hair and eyes were black. She was lithe and young, but not a girl, more of a woman. She was also startlingly beautiful, with perfect, even white teeth that showed through her smile, and perfect features. The third time she said his name, as she was stepping from her dinghy to the deck, he answered. By then he was awake. By then, too, he was over his surprise.

'Yes, I'm J. G. Hewlett,' he said, beginning to push up off the deck, shiny with salt-spray and perspiration, ten shades darker than she was.

She stood upon the deck rolling with the pitch and sway of his boat, smiling like a child. 'You are a hard person to find, Mr Hewlett.'

He watched the breeze flatten her white dress against large round breasts, pull it taut at the curve and flare of strong, graceful hips, and half arose into a sitting position.

She laughed. 'I love the sea. Even at anchor, I love it. You must also love it, Mr Hewlett.' She walked towards him. 'Do you know who I am, Mr Hewlett?'

He answered with a smile. 'Sure. With the sun behind you like that, with your hair tumbling, with a smile that could launch a thousand ships—you're the Lady of the Sea.'

He arose, pulled over a small deck-chair for her, and glanced around among the other tethered small craft. There was no one upon any of the other decks. Not that it would matter. He eased back down upon the deck, bare-chested, with the battered cotton hat turned down all around, and gazed up at her. She was enough to inspire poetry in a man who couldn't even write a three-line limerick.

'Astarte,' she said, and laughed into his eyes.

He pondered that a moment before commenting. 'Benedict and Fleisher would have a fit. I'm not supposed even to know what you look like.'

'Benedict and Fleisher were the ones who told me you owned this boat. Your secretary wouldn't tell me anything.'

Jim gently nodded. 'Benedict and Fleisher sent you, then.'

'Oh no. They only told me your address and about this boat. I didn't go to the address. On a day like this, you would find a man near the water. That's what I told myself. So—I came down here, borrowed some binoculars from a man who rents small boats, saw you lying on the deck, rented the little boat and rowed out. Very simple, no?'

'Very simple,' he echoed. 'Mrs Rumi—'

'Astarte.' The black eyes looked steadily at him. 'Do you mind?'

He didn't mind in the slightest. 'Astarte. You blew it for Benedict and Fleisher. Did you know that? I mean, you put things on a person-to-person level between you and me, and Benedict and Fleisher don't like that. They're a very prestigious nest of legal eagles. They don't really consider private investigators on their level. I am a work-horse, to them, you see, and work-horses aren't supposed to fraternise with their clients.'

She had absolutely no accent at all, and for a woman who had to be among the richest in the world, she was as natural as the girl in the cafe down the street from his office. Well; until recently she must have been among the wealthiest women in the world, anyway.

While he studied her, intrigued and curious, she said, 'No, I didn't—blow it—for Benedict and Fleisher, because Mr Benedict himself told me this morning that their Mr Hollingsworth had reported that you were probably not going to help me. So—what more can I lose?'

'Does Mr Benedict or Mr Hollingsworth know that you came down here?'

'No.' She laughed again. 'Not down *here*. Mr Hollingsworth knew I was going to your office, then to your residence. But not down here. Mr Benedict was not in the office when I finally got down there to ask for your address.'

35

Jim finally stopped looking at her. 'I see. And now that you're here . . . I have a bottle of champagne down in the food locker.'

The smile remained when she declined. 'No thank you, Mr Hewlett. If I had a bathing suit I might go swimming. But I don't have one.' She immediately held up a hand. 'Possibly another time. Not today.' She lowered the hand. 'Mr Hewlett . . . ?'

He knew what was coming and leaned with his bare shoulders against the polished railing. 'Do you know why I came down here today, Astarte? I'll tell you; because I think there's something about your embezzlement case that doesn't quite mesh.'

Her smile dwindled, but the black eyes never left his face. 'You have all the particulars. Mr Hollingsworth told me that he gave you—'

'Astarte, there are blank spaces, and there are riddles, and to be very frank, I'm not convinced Hamid Rumi tried to kill you.'

She leaned a little. 'Would you care to see the scar?' He smiled at her. 'No. Well; maybe I'd *like* to, but that wouldn't really settle anything would it?'

'Then you think I lied. Is that it?'

He watched her raise a hand to hold back cascading waves of thick black hair, when a light breeze blew from the north. She *was beautiful*! 'I think something hasn't been told, let's put it that way. And I think, before I go to

Canada and get embroiled with something I may not be able to handle, I should know about all there is to know. No secrets.'

'The fee, then . . . ?'

'Never mind the fee,' he replied. 'It's fine. To be perfectly honest with you, the fee is more money than I've made in all my years at this business put together. Twice as much, to be frank about it. It's not the fee. I just don't want to go busting up to Canada to pull someone else's chestnuts out of the fire—only perhaps to get all my fingers burned off in the process.'

She leaned back, unsmiling now. 'Ask. You want to know, then ask!'

He grinned at her sudden change in mood. Now, the black eyes bored at him, demanding and a little imperious. He continued to grin as he said, 'Where did you get a hundred million dollars, Astarte?'

'From my father, who died six years ago, when I was twenty-two years old. He came out of the war a rich man, don't ask me how he did that, because he never told me, and I didn't ever ask. But that was not how he became *so very* wealthy. He bought land, hill land which was not very valuable at the time. It became very valuable later.'

Hewlett said, 'Opium land?'

'Yes. But not when he owned it. He sold it for millions, and the combine which bought it, developed it into opium land. It was the worst farm land in my country, when he bought it, but it had the exact climate, and the exact kind of stony, well-drained land, for farmers to plant opium flowers. He made millions. The association which bought it made many more millions, and they are making more millions every year.' She stared defiantly at Hewlett. 'Is that it, Mr Hewlett—because my wealth came from opium land, you have refused to—?'

'I haven't refused to do anything, Astarte. I'm just being cautious. May I ask another question?'

'Ask!'

'How long were you married to Hamid Rumi?'

'One year. We were married in Athens, which is where I met him. He is an official of the Turkish government now. Do you know how that came about? I bought him the position!'

'You were stabbed from behind, were you not?'

'Yes!'

'Then how could you identify your attacker, Astarte?'

The black eyes flashed fire. 'My husband has a scar on the back of his left hand, Mr Hewlett. He also wears—at least he used to wear—a very expensive diamond and white-platinum ring I gave him. He reached around to cover my mouth with his left hand. I recognised the hand. Then he stabbed me from behind with his right hand.'

Jim looked out across the breakwater where the sun was balancing, red and huge, in the far distance. The damned police report had mentioned none of this. He looked back at her. 'Is it possible that your husband could have paid someone to minimise your statement about the attack?'

She showed scorn. 'Possible? Mr Hewlett, Hamid Rumi already had friends among the people in the opium trade, as well as in the army. He wouldn't have had to bribe anyone, but of course he did. Not just about the attempted murder. How do you suppose he could inherit from me so swiftly? Two days after I was reported dead, Hamid Rumi owned everything my father had left me. In just *two* days. Isn't that unusual?'

Jim did not answer. He knew nothing about Turkish law. In the US it would not only have been unusual, it would also have been impossible. He asked her one more question.

'How did you get to America?'

'I was very ill, in the fishing village. They only knew that I was a woman. They did not know who I was. Even their doctor had no idea. He was the one who brought me newspapers while I was recovering. It was all there, in the papers. I didn't have to be brilliant to know what would happen if I returned to Ankara. You can buy an assassin's services in Turkey very cheaply, Mr Hewlett

. . . I sold my ring and my bracelet, bought passage to the United States, and came here.'

'Without a passport, Astarte?'

Her smiled returned, but bitter now. 'I had a passport, Mr Hewlett. I told you—in Turkey money speaks very eloquently. It was a forgery.'

Jim got to his feet. 'It speaks pretty eloquently here, too, sometimes.' He offered his hand. 'Come along. I'm hungry.' She went with him down into the little cabin below decks.

Chapter Five

Clarence Bryson telephoned the following morning with the information he had ferreted out. The CIA knew Hamid Rumi. It also knew he was due to arrive in Canada very shortly, with that Turkish trade Commission, but most importantly, from Jim Hewlett's viewpoint, was the background information they had on the man. The CIA dossier was much more detailed than anything Jim had been able to come up with on Hamid Rumi. According to Bryson, Rumi had captained a kind of constabulary unit whose function was discreetly to police the opium-growing enclaves, pick up reports from farmers and others in the countryside, of strangers, and to carry out orders from his superiors in the shadow government, which very often included orders to commit assassination.

Startlingly, the CIA knew all the details of the attempted murder of Astarte, and it had information on the demise of Hamid Rumi's first wife, the French woman, which no other source seemed to possess; at least Jim Hewlett had been led to believe no such detailed particularity existed.

The Frenchwoman had been murdered, according to what Bryson's CIA contact told him, by strangulation, and had been flung into the sea, but this time no cold water revived her, and no fishing boat happened by to save her, which could not have happened in any case; the CIA report showed that the woman had not a drop of water in her lungs. She had been dead before her body reached the sea.

Finally, Hamid Rumi was suspected of having close ties with a very select and very secret society of Turkish assassins, supposedly of very ancient origin. It was one of those associations which had come down through the centuries, never large, never altogether influential even in its own country, let alone elsewhere, which most nations possessed. But, like the Ku-Klux Klan in the United States, Hamid Rumi's select society of assassins had a hard core. No one doubted that. It had a hard core of genuine assassins, perhaps no more in number of fifty or sixty, and they were not identifiable, but they undoubtedly existed, and, unlike the ritualised, formal brotherhood, these genuine *hashashin,* descendants of the original founders of the society, were quite dedicated to silent murder.

The CIA report had been unable to come up with a membership list of this group, and therefore had been unable to say categorically that Hamid Rumi belonged to it, but if circumstantial evidence meant anything, he did. A number of the murders he had 'investigated' as part of the Turkish constabulary corps, had been commited in the exact, traditionalised manner, of the assassins, and Hamid Rumi's official reports had consistently concealed this fact.

If he didn't actually belong, then, he was certainly sympathetic to the secret group.

Jim Hewlett was curious about the details of these ritual murders, about the precise manner in which they were committed—such as, perhaps, reaching round front with the left hand to cover the mouth, and plunging in the dagger, possibly in some unique manner, with the right hand. For example, the scar on Astarte's back showed that the knifeblade had described a half circle, like a crescent, either before it had been tilted down so that the tip sliced through the flesh and muscle, or afterwards. At the time he saw her scar, he had only noted this peculiarity, but today, after his conversation with Clarence Bryson, he recalled it more vividly, wondering whether or not it was a kind of trademark—and perhaps also a warning—recognisable by those who privately knew of the existence of this secret society of assassins.

If it was a warning, it would probably be adequate to prevent knowledgeable Turks from aiding anyone bearing that mark, should a victim so marked, manage to survive as Astarte had done. And this, of course, would bear out something she had told him last night: That if she went to the Turkish consulate with an appeal for help, she would be putting herself in as much jeopardy as she would be doing if she returned to Turkey seeking justice.

An hour after he had talked to Bryson, he telephoned Carl Hollingsworth to bring round the cheque and pick up the signed agreement. Then he and Mary Friday had coffee in the small file room off the reception room, and Mary sweetly asked if a woman who had been trying to locate him yesterday, had found him.

He did not meet her gaze when he answered that the woman had found him on his boat down in Santa Monica harbour.

'Would she, by any chance, have anything to do with the Benedict and Fleisher assignment, then, *Mr* Hewlett?'

When Jim looked up, Mary Friday's liquid dark eyes had the bright, feline expression of a hunting tigress. He smiled at her. 'She has *everything* to do with Benedict and Fleisher,' he told her. I've agreed to the assignment. We'll start a file—and call it simply, Astarte.'

Mary re-filled his cup as she said, 'Oh yes. Astarte—One night she went naked down into hell, didn't she?'

He waited for her to look up from re-filling his cup, but she did not meet his gaze, she simply replaced the pot upon the small hot-plate and turned slightly to gaze out the window.

Carl Hollingsworth arrived. They heard someone enter from the hallway, and went into the reception-room where Hollingsworth smiled, a trifle guardedly, Hewlett thought, as he extended his hand, then followed Jim into the private office.

Hewlett took the envelope with the signed agreement in it from a desk drawer and tossed it across in front of Benedict and Fleisher's man. Hollingsworth withdrew the document, glanced only at the last page, saw the signature, pocketed the agreement, and passed over an envelope with the fifty thousand dollar cheque in it. He stood a moment studying big Jim Hewlett, then he said, 'I am to tell you that in the event of trouble, Benedict and Fleisher will be in the background, prepared to do whatever can legally be done.'

Jim laughed. 'Legally? That kind of assurance isn't worth much, is it?'

Hollingsworth's smooth face showed nothing, even though he probably felt resentment. 'Well; our position is clear-cut in this affair. We represent Astarte, which means we will also represent you, since you'll also be working for that same person. There is one element Mr Benedict and I discussed last evening . . . We can't be expected to jeopardise the firm's long-standing respectability if something of an international nature arises. You understand that, I'm sure.'

Jim understood perfectly. He also understood something that Carl Hollingsworth probably hadn't considered, which was, simply, that James Garfield Hewlett was making a departure from the rules he had established for himself the day he became a professional private investigator. If Hollingsworth *had* understood this, he would certainly have attributed it to the fee; the reasonable assumption of any Establishment man like Carl Hollingsworth, was always that ethics and standards, pure and lofty as they were, could be reached best by building a monument of money beside their pillar, and when the top was reached—which differed from man to man—ethics and standards got smothered by the greenbacks.

There was nothing wrong with that notion, except that in this particular case, it was the wrong notion. Prim, precise, cold-blooded Carl Hollingsworth would probably never have understood the *real* reason Jim Hewlett had finally handed over the signed agreement.

As they stood facing one another across the desk, Jim Hewlett's smile came up. He opened the envelope, looked at the cheque, tossed them both upon the desktop and said, 'She blew the Astarte-cover, didn't she?'

Hollingsworth understood perfectly. 'She's our client, not our employee, Mr Hewlett. In any event, she succeeded where we failed, but according to Mr Benedict, it's to end there. Until this affair is settled satisfactorily, it'll be the firm's responsibility to see that she's kept safe. Mr Benedict himself, has engaged private quarters for her, and no one but he and I will see her. You, of all people will appreciate this kind of precaution.'

'Sure,' smiled Jim Hewlett. 'If anything happens to Astarte—there goes Benedict and Fleisher's fee right out the damned window.'

'Mr Hewlett, sometimes you make it a little difficult for me to like you.'

Jim laughed. 'Care for some coffee? *Turkish* coffee.'

'No, thank you.' Hollingsworth buttoned his jacket. 'You have our company telephone number. We would like it if you'd call in now and then while you're up north. Mr Benedict is very interested in this affair. In fact, he told me last night the firm's never had anything exactly like this, on its hands before.'

'You tell Mr Benedict that if I call your people, it won't be every few days to report, it'll be just one call—to tell you to run for cover because I'm caught. By the way, did you know Hamid Rumi is probably a member in good standing of a secret society of assassins?'

Hollingsworth did not look surprised. 'There *was* something in the report . . . I'm not really very surprised.'

'Well, the reason I mentioned it, friend, is because if they nail me, and find out who sent me, you and Mr Benedict might not be in the best positions you've ever been in, in your lives. I don't know that those lads go fanning out after employers, but I'd guess that the possibility exists.'

Carl Hollingsworth gazed a trifle pensively at Jim Hewlett as he replied. 'Isn't that a little fantastic, Mr Hewlett?'

Jim smiled. 'It's fantastic all right. This whole thing is a little fantastic.'

When Carl Hollingsworth departed, after one of his conferences with Jim Hewlett, he usually did so looking impassive. Today was no exception.

After he was gone Jim rang for Mary Friday. They began working up a file on the Astarte assignment. Jim dictated, Mary Friday wrote, and although she looked up in wonder a time or two, an hour later when they had it worked into a good sequence and she departed to do the typing, she turned in the doorway and said, 'Overnight you've become one of those 007 types, Mr Hewlett; immense fee, cloak-and-dagger—mostly dagger—intrigue, and . . . of course an exquisite woman.' She smiled her sweetest smile at him. 'I said—overnight.' She closed the door and went out to her desk, leaving him to gaze thoughtfully at the back of the closed door.

For a while he did nothing, just sat there, feet cocked up, gazing at the flawless blue sky beyond his streetside window. Mary had the cheque to deposit. By the time it cleared, a matter of a couple of days, he would be preparing to fly north to British Columbia. It was a nice beginning. Not that he questioned the integrity of a Benedict and Fleisher cheque, but it was nice to know all that money was at his disposal, *before* he planed out to earn it.

The temptation was very strong to return to the sailboat and do nothing for the remainder of this day, except that something would be missing. He considered this objectively, and it occurred to him that every time he returned to his sailboat from now, something would be missing, and he would be reminded of it.

The boat was his escape. It did not even belong to the same world, the same atmosphere, it didn't even live in the same air or sunshine. That's what every man needed, a private place where he could shed his routine skin the way serpents shed their skin. It amounted to some kind of inner regeneration.

The danger was that escape and regeneration became gradually as important as the other thing. In time, it was quite conceivable that they would become *more* important.

He sighed, stood up from the desk and mentally worked out the flight itinerary from Los Angeles to Vancouver. He also considered the advantages of going up there ahead of schedule, in order to have a few days to familiarise himself with the terrain, and whatever else might provide the endemic background he would be functioning against— such as the buildings he would have to know when the trade commission arrived.

There was no schedule, in the strict sense. *He* would not inaugurate the action, in any case, that would be done by the arrival and subsequent movements, of Hamid Rumi. All he would do would be to pick the exact spot and the exact time. More than likely, he would have to decide upon several spots where the confrontation could be effected, and also several times for it to occur.

There was also the principal objective to be considered. Should he try and effect the meeting *before* Hamid Rumi visited a Canadian bank for the purpose of putting his wealth in safe keeping, or should he allow this to happen, and subsequently to create opportunity for their meeting *after* the Turk was confident and relaxed?

He cracked his knuckles, and decided for the time being to allow intrigue to languish while he went out for a bite to eat.

Chapter Six

The flight north was from Los Angeles Municipal Airport by way of Portland, Oregon, then Seattle, Washington, and finally, with seawater off the left wing of the aircraft, across the international boundary into British Columbia, to the most English city of the North American continent—Vancouver.

There were two Vancouvers, one was the island facing the Pacific and separated from the mainland by a wide, river-like body of water called Georgia Strait, and there was the city of Vancouver, facing the Strait. The city was very cosmopolitan, had squares of Elizabethan buildings, parks—even pigeons by the legion—adequate in all ways to make the most confirmed Londoner feel at home.

There was a third Vancouver, an environ of the great city, called North Vancouver, but being contiguous it hardly deserved a separate appelation.

The city's weather was brisk, even in summertime. In wintertime it would have made any Londoner feel at home with its sea-scent, wan winds and fog.

It also happened to be one of the most industrialised cities in the entire continental northwest, with a noticeable separation between its commercial and industrial areas, and its residential areas.

In another way, it put one in mind of London. Amid all the indications of an English affinity, there were innumerable French restaurants. One of these places provided Jim Hewlett with a meal, a secluded table, and the privacy to study his Vancouver city map, the late afternoon of his arrival in British Columbia.

He learned the difference between French restaurants in Vancouver and 'French' restaurants in Los Angeles. In Vancouver they seemed to use English as a second language, and anything on the menu in French, was expected to be ordered in that tongue. Jim Hewlett's one year of highschool Spanish did not help, but he smiled his way past the difficulty, and was rewarded with an understanding smile in turn. Then he ordered in English.

He spent two leisurely days familiarising himself with the city. He had the name of the hotel where the trade commission was to stay, the Dunhill, and he also familiarised himself with the Hotel Dunhill from the inside as well as from the outside. He strolled the entire neighbourhood, even learned the back-alley approaches to the Dunhill from his hotel, the Claridge. The distance was not very great, which was a stroke of good fortune.

A plain girl with a magnificent smile who was in the employ of the city for the purpose of aiding sightseeing foreigners, told him where the trade commission would meet, and even gave him a brochure on the burgeoning economy of Vancouver, its attractive tax shelters for investors, and even included a suggestion that if he anticipated trouble finding his way about, she was sure her agency would be able to come up with someone to guide him.

He affected to read no suggestion into her kindliness, and got back out into the pedestrian traffic to catch a taxi and make a dry-run at the very impressive government building, where trade commissions conducted their business.

He familiarised himself with this building, too, and the area for roughly a mile around it. He even engaged an elderly Scot who had a custodial position in the building, in genial conversation, and was told that a Turkish delegation was coming shortly, to discuss expanded trade with Canada, and during the course of this revelation, the craggy old Scot narrowed a keen eye at Hewlett and said, 'What'll they have in mind trading us, I wonder? Belly-dancers and shepherd's horns, laddie?'

Hewlett laughed, and charmed the old man as he almost invariably was able to do with strangers. 'Whatever it'll, be, if I were a Canadian trade commissioner, I'd keep my eye on the foreign-aid funds.'

The old Scot's face brightened perceptibly. 'Aye. We think alike on that. Let 'em *do* something for it. Let 'em *work* like we do, as have to put up that money through damned-awful tax, I say!'

Hewlett heartily agreed, then he ambled through the vast building with the old Scot's silent blessing, saw the gleaming chambers where lofty international conferences were held, stood a long while before magnificent oil portraits of Canadian officials, mostly departed he assumed, and after completing his personal tour, returned to the bright sunshine outside, and stood a while in the shade of a large tree studying the parking area, the great length of kerbing out front, and the nearby store-fronts, partially concealed by an almost constant ebb and flow of pedestrian traffic. It appeared that more people walked, in Vancouver, than walked in Los Angeles. A good, healthy pastime. He approved, and went along in search of his taxi, then cruised back to within several squares of the Claridge, paid the hack off, and did a little walking himself, right on past the elegant brass and glass front entrance to the Claridge, and on down the street as far as a small bar. There, in an atmosphere which was quaint and cool, and not at all crowded, he ordered a Bloody Mary, took it to a small table, and for a half hour sat in quiet thought, absorbing the knowledge of the city he had been assiduously acquiring without seeming to.

He was satisfied, so far. He still had another few days, and by that time, when the Turkish trade commission arrived, he was confident he'd know the city even better, but basically, he'd know all that area between the Dunhill Hotel, and the government building where the talks would be held.

Beyond that, he still had to gain a rudimentary familiarity with Vancouver banks, but as for any particular bank, that would have to wait until the trade commission arrived.

He returned to his suite at the Claridge, showered, changed, and resumed his orientation course that night by having a good dinner, early, then including in his crash-course of familiarisation, half a dozen night spots. In one of these he met a very handsome, long-legged woman in her thirties with high cheekbones, wide, violet eyes, and a white-gold wedding band. They danced, once. He bought her two drinks, learned that her name was Macmillan, that she did not want to discuss anything else about herself, which probably meant that her husband was out of the city on business, and by midnight when he was ready to leave, Mrs Macmillan was ready to leave with him.

He eluded her without much difficulty, taxied back to the Claridge, and turned in, having discovered one bistro he would thereafter avoid. Probably without much actual sacrifice, since Vancouver had a very lively and widespread nightlife.

By the fourth day, when he picked up a newspaper in the hotel lobby and noticed a concise, matter-of-fact article announcing the arrival in Vancouver of a Turkish trade commission, Jim Hewlett had completed his crash-course, and in general was sufficiently familiar with the bustling, energetic city to find his way around, but he was especially well-orientated in the areas he considered critical to his purpose for being in Canada.

That evening he called Mary Friday at her apartment. She sounded enormously relieved to hear his voice. In fact she said, 'Why haven't you called in before? It's been *days*!'

He laughed at her. 'Don't worry. I left orders at the bank that they are to issue your cheque every Friday morning, for a year.'

'A *year*! How long do you expect to be gone, then?'

He had no idea. 'Maybe a week, maybe two weeks. Honestly, I haven't the foggiest idea. What's new in the lion compound?'

'The office? Well; there are several important letters, and we've had enquiries from three law firms about your availability. Mr Hewlett, I really think you should give some serious thought to bringing in a partner. Well—at least someone else who can go on assignments. All this business slipping away isn't good for the company . . . Is it?'

His answer was tolerant. 'Friday, you nag a lot. Has anyone ever told you that? You're like a wife, no matter how hard a man works or how successful he is, you believe that under your aegis a man could do better.'

She flared up at him. 'I don't think any such thing, and I've never nagged. Not you, nor anyone else. Mr Hewlett, you can run the agency . . .'

'But you also have the most beautiful, soft brown eyes, and the most lovely complexion, I ever saw in a woman . . . Friday?'

'I'm here . . . You just knocked all the wind out of me.'

'I think you're right. Joking aside, I think you're right about bringing in another agent.'

'I wasn't joking. I take down the names and the addresses, and sit there, after I put up the telephone, feeling terribly frustrated.'

'Why? Because of all that business sliding by?'

She said, 'Exactly.' Then she changed her tone, and the subject, by saying, 'You know, Mr Hewlett, you calling me at home like this—when I'm on my own time—is different from us being in the office. You realise that, don't you?'

He realised it, of course, but he was also mystified by this sudden change in her. 'It is different,' he cautiously conceded.

'Then I'm entitled to more familiarity, aren't I?'

He began to suspect something. 'You're entitled to more familiarity. But I warn you, I'm not going to make love by long distance rates. It's just too expensive.'

She cut across that statement almost before he had finished, with a question. 'Is . . . Are you alone, up there in Vancouver?'

The light burst. He was terribly tempted to feign contrition and confess that he had brought along a troupe of Gypsy dancing girls. Instead, he said, 'I am so alone, up here, Friday, that even when I talk to myself, I don't even get any answers. And what kind of a question is that, anyway?'

She answered in a clearly troubled tone. 'Well; it's just that I wondered. About that woman who hunted you down at the marina— on your sailboat—is all.'

He said, 'Has anyone called from Benedict and Fleisher?'

'No, Mr Hewlett. Not a word.'

'Good night, Friday.'

He put down the telephone, looked at his wrist, decided that what he needed next was a hearty seafood meal, then a trip to the trade commission building, and after that it was all in the hands of—someone.

Vancouver was a city where seafood meals were commonplace, and also very good. Hewlett was no connoisseur, but when he chose a particular restaurant, mid-way between his hotel, and the other one, the

Hotel Dunhill, he made his selection on the basis that the front windows were sparkling clean, the dining-room was spacious, the waiters were immaculate, and if there was a better way to choose a dining place in an alien city, he had no idea what it was.

The shock came halfway through his meal when five men entered the restaurant with a look to them Hewlett would have called Sephardic, and which would have been incorrect, except in the context of his meaning; they were swarthy men, with black hair and very dark eyes, but except for one fat man, they had aquiline features, and, again, except for the fat man, who was pudgy-faced with blue eyes and thinning mouse-coloured hair, they were lean, capable-looking, foreigners.

The shock arose when Hewlett raised his eyes at the precise moment one of the swarthy men turned slowly and glanced squarely in Hewlett's direction. Their eyes met, held for a moment, then the black-haired, dark-eyed man's gaze drifted elsewhere round the large room, which was roughly two-thirds full of diners.

Hewlett felt the tingling effect of that sudden meeting of eyes, for moments after the foreigner had satisfied his curiosity, and had taken his seat with his back to Hewlett. For almost two weeks he had been immersing himself in the background of the man he had just locked glances with.

He would have known Hamid Rumi anywhere in the world. The fact that they had just met across an immaculate dining-room in a city neither of them, in all probability, had ever visited before, when neither of them could possibly have expected this meeting, was certainly a surprise, but for Jim Hewlett, it had to be a lot more. He had come a long distance, had painstakingly worked out several optional procedures for the pursuance of his purpose in being in Canada, and had been leisurely preparing himself for whatever was to ensue, with a good supper, prior to seeking out his man, or at least a glimpse of his man, all the while holding the initiative in the palm of his hand—and here was his man, no more than fifty feet from him, under circumstances Hewlett would never have anticipated.

It made him uneasy. If Fate was dealing herself a hand in this affair, was pushing Hamid Rumi at Hewlett, was seeking raffishly to speed things up, then Hewlett had another adversary, one no man ever successfully contended against and *that* was enough to make anyone uneasy.

Chapter Seven

For an active, resourceful man, there were advantages to being spared additional orientation. Half a week alone in an alien city was long enough for anyone. It was certainly long enough for Jim Hewlett.

He was quite prepared to go exploring in the vicinity of the Dunhill, now that he knew the trade commission had arrived, and it helped, too, that although the trade commissioners had arrived earlier than Jim had expected them, shortly after eating at the restaurant, they set off upon a sight-seeing excursion, still accompanied by that pale-eyed fat man, who was probably an official guide, or something, supplied by the Canadian government. It seemed that the trade commissioners did not want to waste a single moment of their visit to Canada, and while they were making certain that they saw as much as possible, even on their first day in the country, Jim Hewlett tested his orientation, and his hastily-created and therefore presumably fragile, private network, by stopping at a small tobacconist's store near the Dunhill, buying a packet of smokes, a newspaper, and asking the elderly, spry and bird-like proprietor if he was aware that a delegation of Turks had recently arrived across the street.

The older man's small eyes twinkled. 'As I've told you, my business is the store, selling merchandise, but my hobby is everything that happens close by. Yes, I knew about those foreigners. I read of it in the newspaper, in fact. Then I saw them arrive over there, bag and baggage, five of them.'

Hewlett turned on his charming smile. 'I think one of them, the fat man, is probably a guide, or something like that, supplied by the government.'

'Ah, yes, of course,' said the tobacconist. 'Well, I didn't get that close a look, you understand.'

Hewlett was completely understanding. Then he said, 'I met them down the street at a restaurant. I mean, I saw them down there.'

'Oh yes, indeed,' stated the wispy, bird-like older man, 'I don't believe they were inside the hotel more than perhaps fifteen minutes. In the restaurant, you say; well, it must have been a long trip.'

Hewlett paid, strolled outside, considered the soaring facade of the Dunhill, and decided that if all the time one needed to settle-in, over there, was about a quarter of an hour, then they probably had not been assigned one of the rear, top-floor apartments or suites, and strolled along to the first cross-street so that he could test another facet of his private network.

Behind the hotel, in an alley which seemed never entirely devoid of shadows, there was a small, marked-off private parkway, apparently only used by very special residents of the Dunhill. There were exactly thirty parking slots for cars back there, and today, there was one more car than there usually was. It would have been conspicuous to someone like Jim Hewlett without having studied the parking lot previously; it had an 'official' car's maple-leaf licence plate, and it was shinier than any of the other half-dozen or so vehicles parked back there. It was standing in a slot marked with hotel symbols which coincided with the number of each floor inside the hotel. So—the commissioners were staying on the third floor. There was nothing to signify which suite of rooms they had, but Hewlett was satisfied, and turned to resume his stroll—when a curly-headed, black-eyed man who had been watching Hewlett from a metal-sheathed, recessed doorway, stepped forth and approached.

For Jim, whose reaction was instantaneous chagrin at having allowed himself to be caught like this, the stranger was identifiable as one of the men from the restaurant, which meant, of course, that this one was not so much a trade commissioner, as he was some kind of security agent.

Jim nodded at the lithe, muscular stranger, fished out his packet of smokes, ripped it open, selected one, and offered one to the Turk. The man's black eyes were hooded and cautiously hostile as he declined in excellent English.

'No thank you. Is one of those cars yours?'

The question offered an easy way out, but Jim smilingly shook his head; any agent worth his salary already knew to whom each of those cars had been registered. He had no illusions about the capability of this muscular Turk.

'No, and that's the trouble,' he said genially. 'I live on the ninth floor. I'm in the marine hardware line. I've tried to get them to assign me one of those parking slots. This is a hell of a city to find parking places in. It wastes a man's time, not just trying to find a place to park, but also, once you've found a place, in making you walk a half mile or so from wherever you've been able to leave your car, to your business appointments, or back here to the hotel.'

The black-eyed man kept watching Hewlett as he listened. 'On the ninth floor,' he said. 'What is your name?'

'Carling. Frank Carling.' Hewlett gazed at the stranger. 'You're with the hotel, then?'

The Turk ignored Jim's question. 'Frank Carling?'

'Yes.'

The Turk stood motionless, facing Hewlett. 'Would you mind stepping inside the registry with me, Mr Carling?'

64

Jim dropped the cigarette. 'What for?'

'I only want to see that your name is listed among the occupants of the ninth floor. It will only take a moment.' The Turk did not smile.

Jim's smile dwindled. 'I'm afraid you'll have to take my word for it. Who are you, anyway?'

'I'm with the Turkish trade commission, Mr Carling.'

'I see. Some kind of policeman?'

The Turk's unwavering black stare was black and hard and unrelenting. He nodded his head.

Jim guessed what was going to happen, and loosened his stance as he repeated what he'd already said, 'If you were a Canadian policeman, I'd go along, but not this time. You can verify who I am without me.'

The Turk did not hesitate. He evidently was accustomed to being obeyed. He took one forward step—and Jim Hewlett eluded his reach with no difficulty, and started to turn as though to walk on down the alley, but the Turk was no novice. He moved immediately to block Jim's progress. Jim halted, looked at the man, and said, 'I wouldn't do this if I were you.'

The Turk came in fast, head up, arms rising. He was clearly a professional. Jim did not retreat, which was the normal procedure, he instead slipped sideways just enough to compel the Turk to twist his body, to manoeuvre himself off-balance, then Jim reached, caught the man's sleeve, pulled his arm down and in, caught the arm at the wrist, and completely turned his body as he swept the man's arm high, and brought it down squarely upon Hewlett's shoulder, at the same time, bending and levering his considerable weight, into the move. The astonished Turk was lifted off his feet, was pulled abruptly against Jim's back, which was braced, then the man came bodily up over the shoulder, and down, hard, upon the pavement of the alleyway. He landed on his back, eyes momentarily glazed from the landing, then he rolled, and Jim released his arm after the throw and take-down.

The Turk got over onto all fours and Jim stepped in, balancing on one foot. The Turk saw it coming, may even have anticipated the kick. He flung out both arms and legs to drop flat, beneath the kick, and at the last moment Jim relented, and did not lash out. Instead, he spoke.

'I told you—in your boots I wouldn't try it.'

The Turk craned around, looking upwards. He waited a moment, then got to his feet, eyes blazing, stepped back and looked down at his soiled clothing, then up again, his face harshly set. 'You're no hardware salesman,' he snarled.

Jim gestured. 'Just walk back on up the alley, and that will be the end of it.'

The Turk continued to glare. 'You were going to wire the car with bombs,' he exclaimed, and Jim was taken by surprise with this accusation.

'You're out of your mind,' he retorted. 'Look,' he held his jacket wide open with both hands. 'See any bombs?' He let the jacket fall back.

The Turk began to brush himself off. 'But you're no hardware salesman, whoever you are,' he growled, beginning to recover his self-control.

Jim did not argue, he simply pointed. 'Walk on out of here.'

The Turk finished adjusting his tie and coat, black eyes fixed on Hewlett. Then he abruptly turned and without another word, began walking. Jim cursed himself, to himself, while watching his attacker depart.

Maybe it wasn't his fault, but whether it was or not he had dropped a clod in the churn this time. Possibly the humiliated bodyguard, or whatever he was, would be too chagrined to mentioned his encounter with the man in the back alley, but that was nothing to rely on, so, whatever interpretation the Turks put on this meeting in the alley, whether they decided someone was deliberately stalking them, or whether they simply decided their security man had run into a citizen who could look out for himself, they were going to be wary henceforth, and the minute it turned up that a foreign trade commissioner had been attacked, the Canadian authorities were also going to be interested.

And—there was the lie about a man named

Carling living on the ninth floor of the Dunhill. That would be verified false within the hour, most probably.

Jim left the alleyway walking southward, then changed course for the sake of instinctive prudence, caught a taxi and drove round for a half hour, before returning to the Claridge to shower, change, and go downstairs again, for his evening meal, disgusted with himself, but unwilling to accept the suggestion that he had blown it.

Regardless of the awkward interlude, regardless of whether it had happened or not, he had been convinced, even before leaving Los Angeles, that when the ultimate confrontation with Hamid Rumi occurred, there would be something more to it than mere talk. He was prepared for physical confrontations. He was always prepared for this kind of thing. But he had thought something of this nature, on his current assignment, might not come about until very near the end of the job. Instead, it had happened at the very outset.

The dinner was excellent, the dining-room was crowded, there seemed to be more people present than previously, something which only indirectly recorded itself upon Jim Hewlett's consciousness, and when he heard the unmistakable slurred, ungrammatical accent of Texas at an adjoining table, he decided that holidayers from below the International line were arriving in noticeable numbers, something to be expected every summer, but perhaps more so this summer in Canada, since the disenchantment of US tourists with France and the Middle East was very widespread. He'd read quite an article about that in the *Los Angeles Times* newspaper only a few days before leaving for Canada.

How this might affect him was unclear, nor did he dwell upon it. People in droves, or by the hundreds and by the thousands, were only important to a man like Jim Hewlett, or to anyone in his line of work, as a background. They provided the colour, the dimension, the in-depth, mobile background through which he could best operate. Otherwise, tourists or natives, it did not matter in the least.

He was finishing his meal when he glanced up and saw two burly men, accompanied by a third man, move into the very wide dining-room entry-way, and stand gazing across the room, which was quite full by this time. The two men he noticed first were drably attired, fair, heavily put-together, but the third man he recognised instantly. It was his adversary of the back alley.

How those other two, obviously city detectives, had managed to run him down so fast, was a mystery. It was also surprising. But most of all, it was alarming. He kept his head down, eating, and scanned the third man over there, waiting to see whether the Turk would

69

finally make an identification. He didn't. He looked, and moved into the room a little further, still peering around where people were coming and going, amid a steady sound of conversation, rattling dinnerware, and moving waiters. Then, finally, he turned, joined the pair of Vancouver detectives, and the three of them went back in the direction of the big lobby.

At once, Hewlett arose, dumped some money atop the table and worked his way through the colour and clamour until he had a slanting view of the large, busy foyer. The Turk and his colourless companions were approaching the registration desk.

Jim moved out into the lobby, sought a secluded chair, sat down and watched. The three men at the counter talked briefly with a clerk, then turned and walked out into the evening, by way of the massive brass and glass streetside doors.

Jim did not move for another ten minutes. Evidently, although the local police had run him down, perhaps through a routine manhunt, to the Claridge, they were not quite prepared, as yet anyway, to make a *concerted* manhunt. If this were so, then Jim had perhaps a few hours to get clear. He arose, avoided the desk, went to the bank of lifts and rode up to his floor. The forewarned are the forearmed, or something like that. He stepped out, saw the bulky shadow at the extreme end of the corridor, stepped back into the lift, punched the button and rode to the ground floor again.

Evidently they *were* prepared to make a concerted manhunt, after all!

He walked directly out of the hotel and kept right on walking, until he found a cab.

Chapter Eight

Big-city police were efficient. No one could deny that, least of all someone like Hewlett who was familiar with the methods of the Los Angeles police, but as he was checking in at another hotel, across the city, something more than the efficiency of the Vancouver police troubled him.

Somehow, they knew his identity. Otherwise, they wouldn't have had his floor, his suite, at the Claridge, staked-out. He completed checking in, using the name Robert Harding, went up to his room, and without luggage making a settling-in necessary, he went immediately to the telephone, put in a call to Mary Friday, routed her from her bed, and asked who, if anyone, had been round, or had called, from Benedict and Fleisher.

She answered a trifle fuzzily. 'No one. Do you know what time it is?'

He glanced at his wrist. 'Nine o'clock. *No* one retires at nine o'clock.'

'I did, tonight, and I was asleep.'

'If no one's called from Benedict and Fleisher, has anyone else called to ask if I was out of the city?'

'Yes, there have been a number of calls. I have them tabulated at the office. One man called from Florida, he wanted—'

'I'm not interested in someone from Florida, Friday, I'm interested in how someone down there could have tipped off my identity to some guys up here in Vancouver.'

She was momentarily quiet, then she spoke again, in a fresher-sounding tone of voice. 'Could it have been your alluring playmate from Santa Monica harbour—Astarte?'

'Did she call?'

'A *woman* called, asked if you were available. I presumed she meant were you in the city, and told her you were *not* available. I thought at the time the voice was the same as the woman who called that other time, when you were on your boat. But she left no name, just thanked me and rang off.'

He took the telephone to a sofa, sat down, crossed his legs and frowned. He was working *for* Astarte. She was deathly afraid of her husband. Why would *she* call someone in Vancouver about him?

He said, 'Besides Astarte, who else wanted to know whether I was in the city?'

'I just told you, Mr Hewlett. The list is on my desk at the office. I can't remember them all; there were about seven or eight calls, and they all wanted to speak to you. right away, which is par for the course, isn't it?'

He ignored the question. 'Friday, in the morning I want you to call Hollingsworth, of Benedict and Fleisher, and tell him I called in, and told you I'd be returning within a day or two. Tell him I said something has gone wrong up here, and I'm coming back for a conference with him, with a view to dropping the case. Do you have all that?'

'Yes, Mr Hewlett . . . Has something *really* gone wrong, up there?'

'Yeah. But I'm not coming back. I just want you to make Hollingsworth think I am. I want him to believe I'm discouraged with this case. But do it damned discreetly, Hollingsworth is no fool. Then, tomorrow night, I'll call you again for Hollingsworth's reaction.'

'All right . . . What kind of a reaction should I expect from him?'

'Don't expect anything from him. Don't try to second-guess him. Just let the thing work itself out naturally. Okay?'

'Yes.'

He put down the telephone, gently, sat a moment longer in thought before putting the telephone back upon its little table, then he strolled to a window and gazed out over the vast, glowing skyline of Vancouver, in the direction of the inlet.

Aside, from Mr Benedict, of Benedict and Fleisher, there *should* be only Mary Friday, Carl Hollingsworth, and Astarte, who knew where he was, and *why* he was up in Canada. Friday would not have tipped off anyone. It didn't make any sense for Astarte to do so, either. Hollingsworth did not *seem* to have a valid reason for treachery, either, but of the three, he liked him best for the part.

If he had known the man better, had been able to spend more time with him, perhaps he could have arrived at a more satisfactory conclusion, but for the time being all he thought of was the amount of money involved. Men in much more exalted positions than junior law partners had sold people out in exchange for a fat pocket of money, and he knew for a fact that Carl Hollingsworth did not especially like Jim Hewlett, not that this had to have anything at all to do with selling someone out; the only genuine consideration in a case like that, was the amount of money he might acquire for his treachery, which brought it all right back into focus—any time a hundred million dollars was concerned, *someone* could be depended upon to get cute. The more people involved, the more this could be depended upon.

There was, also, one other consideration. Maybe it was *not* Hollingsworth. Maybe it was none of them. Maybe it was someone he did not know at all. A hundred million pounds of sugar attracted an awful lot of flies. Hewlett could, just off-hand, think of several he didn't know, had never seen, and who weren't even in either the US or Canada. That doctor, for instance, who had nursed Astarte back to life in a small Turkish fishing village. Or one of the fishermen who had fished her from the sea and brought her ashore. They had newspapers in Turkey, exactly as they had them everywhere else. After she had slipped through their fingers, it was entirely possible that they had discovered who she had been, and had also succumbed to greed.

He left the hotel, a third-rate place at best, and went along to a small bar in the neighbourhood for a nightcap. It was not that he needed the drink, any more than he had needed that packet of smokes he'd purchased from the tobacconist. He never drank very much, and although he had lit up a smoke in the alleyway just prior to his physical dispute with the Turk, he did not smoke either; had quit smoking three years earlier, in fact. But being cooped up in the new hotel room left a lot to be desired for an active individual, so he went along to the bar, got comfortable atop a bar stool, and ordered a gimlet, which he sat and sipped, as he came to the conclusion that Fate, blast her anyway, was indeed buying into his little game. He was being pushed towards some kind of unpleasant vortex of trouble a whole lot faster than he liked. Also, he had now lost the initiative.

It would only take the Vancouver police overnight to verify through telecommunications who James G. Hewlett was, what he did for a living, and from there an idiot would be able to guess that his interest in the Turkish trade commission was not trade; at least an idiot would be able to deduce that James G.

Hewlett had not just accidentally happened to arrive in Canada three or four days prior to the trade commission's arrival, had not just accidentally been eyeing the parking lot of the Dunhill, and had not just accidentally lied to the Turk he had trounced, about being someone named Carling.

Whether it could be figured out exactly why he was in Vancouver, interested in the Turks, was problematical—unless, of course, someone like Hollingsworth had tipped either the police, or the Turks, off, and in that case the whole damned ballgame was blown sky high.

He still would not return to Los Angeles.

He ordered his second gimlet, shook loose the attentions of a red-headed woman who came over to make his acquaintance, and tasted the second drink, which was weaker than the first one had been, all the while telling himself that for a hundred thousand dollars—and his pride—he was one hell of a long way from pitching in the towel.

He paid the barman, left the building, went in search of a taxi, and did not find one until he'd walked almost a mile in the clear, brisk, sea-scented night, by which time his adrenalin was flowing again, the way it always did when something was threatening him, challenging him, driving him towards a tough-minded course of action.

He rode to within a few squares of the

Dunhill, paid off the driver, waited until the hack was lost in the diminishing night-time traffic, then strolled as far as the tobacconist's shop, which was closed now, and dark, then he stepped into a doorway and waited. It always took a little time for a man entering a particular environment, with a particular, dominating point of view uppermost in his mind, to blend with the ethos. Not as much time at night as was required in daylight, though.

He finally picked him out.

There was still a fair amount of vehicular traffic, but the pedestrian traffic was almost minimal, and that was part of the ethos, too; it helped Hewlett, who was also stationary, locate the other stationary man over in a layer of night-shadow near the Dunhill's lighted, gleaming front entrance.

There would, of course, be another one round back. There might even be one in the parking lot, and without any question, there would be at least one more, inside the hotel on the floor where the trade commission had its suite of rooms.

The man he could make out in the shadows had the stance, the build, and the cultivated drabness of a city detective. Hewlett was satisfied the man was not one of the Turks. He felt like swearing. With a forewarned police-shield, it would be more difficult to get at Hamid Rumi. Under some circumstances, it might even have been considered downright impossible, but Jim Hewlett rejected any such notion. He did, however, have one gnawing worry. If Hamid Rumi was a man who worried easily, he just might fly out of Canada, and *that* would make Jim Hewlett's job one hell of a lot more difficult, not to mention more dangerous.

This was his paramount cause for anxiety. He was aware of it as he stood, relaxed and easy, watching the watcher over across the roadway, near the front of the hotel. Whatever he did, hereafter, had to be thought-out with this possibility in mind. Whatever he did, hereafter, had to be predicated upon the basis that he had to get at Hamid Rumi with a one-shot success; if he tried to get at the man any other way, he was very likely going to scare him away.

A dark car slid to the kerbing over where that plain-clothesman was standing. Another man alighted, he and the bored-looking individual exchanged brief remarks, then the bored-man climbed into the unmarked police car, which drove away, and the fresh guard took over.

Hewlett had once read a Japanese book on *bushido* in which it said that those who defend, regardless of their superior numbers, are of necessity stationary individuals, while those who attacked, need not be numerous, and actually held the secret of success in their grip, because they alone knew what they were going to do.

Hewlett smiled to himself. That sounded great. And, undoubtedly, it was factual. But in his case, tonight, at any rate, it didn't help a whole lot, because he did not *know* what he was going to.

Then that meddling Fate intervened. He should have become suspicious immediately; so far, that sardonic Fate had not been on his side, and had certainly done him no favours.

Two men sauntered forth, over there. One of them turned aside to speak momentarily to the new guard. Meanwhile, his companion, a sinewy man dressed a little too well and wearing his jet-black, curly hair, a trifle too long, stepped to the edge of the kerbing to light a cigarette beneath a street-lamp, and Jim Hewlett sighed.

It was that same man he'd had the run-in with much earlier out back of the hotel. Hewlett wondered if this individual were the only active commissioner, or if he just *seemed* to be the most restless.

The other man returned, said something, then he and the Turk stepped forth to cross the street. Hewlett had to move at once. They might not turn southward in his direction, but he moved anyway, he strolled down the street for a hundred or so yards, then crossed to the opposite side, and until he turned northward, in the direction of the hotel, he made no attempt to locate the pair of strollers. They had, in fact, turned northward, and were now angling in the direction of a night-club with subdued lighting. As Hewlett ambled along, he saw them enter the bar. If the Turk was expecting something like the night-time activity of a place such as Istanbul, he was in for one of the largest disappointments of his life. Vancouver, after dark, did not resemble either Istanbul, which was the most lively and sophisticated city in Turkey, or Ankara, in central Turkey, which was also slightly frenzied after dark, either by skyline, environment—small, or in its night-life.

Jim Hewlett put those two individuals out of his mind for the time being. The fact that they were together, and out of it, diminished the danger by two, but that was not very encouraging. In fact, it was not encouraging at all, not when there were still the other Turks at the hotel, and an entire deployment of bodyguards between them and Jim Hewlett.

Still, he told himself as he veered off on a side-street which paralleled the south side of the Dunhill hotel, as the old *bushido* authority had said, a guy with a reason to be troublesome, had the fluidity of movement and the initiative, troublesome guys required. Something to that effect.

Chapter Nine

Fate was not one of those things a man could not depend upon, like the weather, political trends, and female willingness.

Jim Hewlett was a square southward of the Dunhill, walking east in search of a taxi, when a slight, fragile—and unmistakable—silhouette loomed ahead, too close for Jim to affect a casual transfer to the opposite side of the street. It was the bird-like tobacconist. He hadn't thought of the man all day, except that brief time when he had passed his shop earlier. There was no critical reason why he should have wanted to avoid the older man, nevertheless he would have preferred to avoid him. Now, he could not do it.

It was a fault, definitely, being recognised in the locale of the Dunhill, at night, in downtown Vancouver, by anyone with whom he was acquainted, even someone he only knew very casually.

The older man halted, put his head slightly to one side, bird-like, and said, 'Well, there's more than one of us needs the night air to clear his sinuses, eh?'

Jim smiled. 'Or to work off his frustrations.'

The bright, bead-like little eyes fastened intently upon Hewlett. 'Did you know there was a police guard at the hotel?'

Jim drawled his response. 'Is that a fact?'

The intent eyes did not waver. 'Could you possibly guess why?'

'Because it's Canadian custom to guard all foreigners?'

'No,' stated the tobacconist, 'because someone attacked one of those Turkish trade people in the alley today.'

Jim's affable smile showed a little surprise. 'Is that so? Did they catch him?'

'No. But they have a description of him. Big, powerful, youngish man.' The older man smiled slyly. 'I heard about it this afternoon. You'd be surprised at the information a man can pick up if he can only keep his eyes open, and listen to talk on the streets.' The tobacconist's shrewd eyes narrowed. 'I have customers from the hotel who've been coming over to my store for years. I'm a good listener.'

Jim didn't doubt that at all, but he wasn't interested in it, either, 'Why would anyone attack trade commissioners; there isn't that much ill feeling towards Turks in Canada, is there?'

The old man cackled. 'I doubt if there's a thousand Canadians who ever saw a live Turk. No, there's no ill-will towards them. Anyway, my informant told me it probably wasn't a Canadian who attacked the man . . . It was an American. A large, powerful, American, wearing a herringbone-tweed jacket like you were wearing when you stopped in for a packet of smokes this morning, and a pair of grey flannel trousers. Coincidence, eh?'

Jim considered the old man. 'Coincidence. I'm like the majority of Canadians—I haven't seen very many Turks, either. At least not in the US or Canada. Herringbone jackets happen to be very big where I come from in the US this season.'

The old man pondered a moment, letting his keen eyes drift briefly away from Hewlett. Then he said, 'Well, it's none of my affair. I'm interested, is all. I'm *not* what James Fraser, the old clot who runs the apothecary's shop next door, calls me, I'm not an old snoop.' The bright little eyes jumped back again. 'As for seeing a Turk, I just saw two of them leaving the alley behind the Dunhill, walking rather quickly, I must say.'

Hewlett cocked an indifferent eyebrow. 'Which direction?'

'Up the alley, northward, in the direction of the parking area. Probably going to take a drive. It's a delightful night, you know.' The small eyes beamed sardonically.

Hewlett thoughtfully considered the tobacconist. He had no reason to favour Jim Hewlett over anyone else. Jim had certainly not become a customer; a newspaper and a packet of smokes couldn't induce loyalty, or even any particular friendship, between a merchant and a one-time customer. But there *was* something between them; he *felt* that in some way they were friends in a manner that had nothing much to do with the tobacconist's store, or, for the matter of that, had nothing actually to do with anything he could think of.

He said, 'Keep an eye open for a man wearing a herringbone jacket who runs around attacking Turks, won't you?' and started past. The little old man halted him with a neighing snicker.

'That's almost what the gentleman from the hotel asked me to do.'

Jim glanced back. 'And you did it?'

The old man soberly inclined his head. Then he snickered again. 'Of course.'

They parted. Jim walked casually as far as the dark maw of the alleyway, then turned to look back. The old man must already have crossed to his shop, or in the direction of some roominghouse close by, because he certainly was no longer in sight.

Jim stepped into the alleyway, strolled slowly up it, and because he had already discovered how handily the Turks were at secreting themselves, he stayed well to the far side as he advanced, watching for shadowy, recessed places.

He did not go up the full distance, to the back of the hotel. He only went as far as he had to go, remaining on the far right side of the alleyway, until he could see into the private parking place.

The shiny dark car with the maple-leaf

licence plate was not in its slot.

He halted, thought a moment, then turned back the way he had come, had almost re-emerged into the street, when a police car, cruising slowly, veered inward slightly as though it meant to halt at sight of someone coming forth from the alleyway, then it kept on going. Jim breathed a sigh of relief, and briskly walked on.

He caught a taxi, drove past the Claridge, where his luggage was, did not even consider trying to retrieve it, went on down to within a few blocks of his present hotel, paid off the hack and went confidently along towards his hotel—and almost walked into another trap.

If it hadn't been for a traffic cruiser, identifiable by colour and the light atop its roof, pausing at the kerbing outside his new hotel, while a uniformed man in the car handed a slip of paper to a plainclothesman standing near the hotel entrance, Jim would have walked into the lobby.

Now, however, he stepped off the kerbing, aimed for a small restaurant approximately opposite the hotel entrance, went in, took a table near the front window, and ordered a meal he had never felt less like eating in his life, and for as long as he could, he toyed with the food, and watched the man across the street.

How they had managed to track him down so efficiently the *second* time, was a mystery.

He did not sit there indefinitely marvelling. As soon as he was satisfied that it was indeed a discreet stake-out, over there, he paid, left the restaurant walking northward, and at the first intersection when he saw an empty hack, he called the driver over, climbed in, and drove north, his intention, this time, to get into a part of the city where they could not trace him—he hoped—for at least two days.

But engaging a room without luggage, in a better part of town, was not so easy. He got by all right by telling a story, with the appropriate expression of disgust, of having only just flown into town, and discovering at the airport that his luggage had gone on to Alaska.

He had a ground floor room, which he was not very enthusiastic about, preferring upper rooms, ones with convenient fire-escapes, but it was getting late and he did not anticipate being tracked down again, at least until morning, so he locked the door behind himself, shed his clothes, took a shower, locked and blocked the door, and went to bed.

Lying in utter darkness, thinking, he decided that there were only two alternatives to his plight; do exactly what he had told Mary Friday he intended to do—enplane for Los Angeles—or stay on, but alter the rules of the game by seizing the initiative again.

He went to sleep satisfied on which he would pursue, and awakened the following day still just as convinced. He had a good breakfast, told the hotel clerk he was going to the airport to see about his luggage, and went instead to the first barber shop for a shave. Then, with the entire day ahead of him, he returned to the vicinity of the Dunhill hotel, by way of the government building where the trade talks were to convene, and entered a haberdashery to purchase a complete second outfit, from the skin out. While the clerk was totalling his purchases, Hewlett strolled to a window, studied the facade of the Dunhill, and immediately picked out the plainclothesman.

He took his purchases back to the hotel in the other sector of town, dressed fresh from the skin out, had lunch, then picked up several local newspapers and returned to his room. He did not go out again until after nightfall. Before that, he searched each newspaper, page by page, and finally found a small announcement on the inside of one paper, announcing that trade talks were in progress. That is all that was said. The Canadian press, at least, was not very favourably impressed by the arrival of a Turkish trade commission. Jim guessed this attitude would have been about the same in the US, where Turkey's resumption of opium cultivation had alienated not only a great proportion of the people, but had also antagonised a great number of government officials.

Finally, when it was close to dinner time and dusk was settling in again, he put through a call to his secretary, and she was not only at home, but she was wide-awake when he identified himself to her, and said, very promptly, that she had talked to Carl Hollingsworth, whose reaction to Jim Hewlett returning before the conclusion of his Canadian assignment, had been one of very noticeable annoyance. In fact, Hollingsworth had told her that, regardless of the agreement between Benedict and Fleisher, and Jim Hewlett, if he threw in the sponge now, and returned, Hollingsworth was going to protest most vigorously to Mr Benedict.

Jim said, 'He meant it?'

Mary Friday's reply was dry. 'I'd say he meant it. In fact, I'd say he got angry. He implied that you might never have intended to fulfil the obligations of the agreement; that you may only have signed the papers in order to get the fifty thousand dollars advance. I think, Mr Hewlett, that he intends to try and persuade Mr Benedict to sue for a return of the money, if you come back, now?'

Jim sighed. There went his best hope of finding the leak. Then Mary Friday deepened the mystery a little by saying, 'A gentleman from the police department dropped by, this afternoon, asking for you, and when I told him you were out of town, he said he knew that, and he wanted you to return, if you were on an assignment for some woman who had called in to the detective bureau saying that your life was in very serious danger every hour you remained in Canada. The detective said he'd been instructed to contact our Department of State, and the FBI, by his superiors, to get you out of Canada immediately by whatever means.'

Jim was baffled. 'He said *a woman* called him?'

Mary Friday answered crisply. 'Yes. I know exactly what you're thinking. I thought the same thing. But would she do that; would she deliberately tip your hand to the local police like that?'

Hewlett did not ask who Mary Friday meant. He said, 'She might, I don't really know. I don't really know her that well.'

'Oh . . . ?' said Mary Friday, drawling the word, then hoisting it to allow it to hang in the air, in the form of a cynical question.

Jim ignored this. 'Look; tell Hollingsworth you have talked to me, and I wanted to speak directly to Astarte—to ask a couple of questions pertinent to what I'm doing up here. Tell him, damn it all, that unless he complies, I *will* chuck it, and his lousy fee along with it.'

'All right. But what am I to—?'

'Just listen, will you, Friday? When you get Astarte on the line, tell her I've called you tonight, and want her to tell you what kind of investments her husband might be interested in, and what bank in Canada he might visit. If she doesn't know the bank, that's all right.

90

That part of your conversation with her is only to get the conversation going. Tell her the Canadians have her husband under twenty-four-hour police guard, and there doesn't seem to be any way to get to him, but that I'll make one more try, about noon tomorrow, then I'll head for the airport and book passage back to Los Angeles in the afternoon. Have you got all that?'

'Yes. It sounds ambiguous, but you'll have your reasons, won't you?'

'I have them,' he replied. 'Contact her first thing in the morning. Okay?'

'Okay.'

'And one more thing. Don't contact Hollingsworth again, but if he happens to call you, tell him I'm staying at the Carleton Arms Hotel in the northern part of Vancouver.'

'I'll tell him, Mr Hewlett . . . Be careful, won't you?'

He smiled, said, 'Indeed I will,' and rang off.

Chapter Ten

The game of entrapment worked both ways. He had set Astarte up so that if she responded to what Mary Friday told her, there would be an increased police guard around Hamid Rumi by morning.

He really thought she had to be the one who was trying to get him caught, and if her motives were altruistic, if she simply wanted him taken by the police in order to prevent his being caught by Hamid Rumi and his companions, and perhaps killed by them, it was very noble of her, but it was also ruining his chances, and he did not like that.

He had also arranged a trap for Carl Hollingsworth, although he did not believe Hollingsworth was the one who was behind the treachery. If Hollingsworth *was* the person working against him, then there would be a clutch of police at the airport, waiting for Hewlett to appear. But best of all, if the police swooped down upon the hotel where he was presently staying, at least until morning, then that would clinch the case against Hollingsworth, since he would be the only person, besides Mary Friday, who would be aware of that.

Of course, the worst part of all this was that it diverted him from his goal and kept him on the defensive. Still, he could do nothing about Hamid Rumi until he knew who was trying to stab him in the back.

He had a good night's sleep, checked out of the hotel before breakfast, found another hotel several miles away, checked in, then hired a taxi and cruised back in the direction of the former hotel.

He had set his traps to allow himself all morning to make a determination concerning the identity of his treacherous friend. But it did not take all morning. The Carleton Arms, where he had spent the previous night, had two unmarked police cars opposite it, parked discreetly a short distance away, but to anyone with Hewlett's background, identifiable for what they were, and it was still actually very early in the morning, which meant, among other things, that Hollingsworth *had* called Mary Friday.

He paid off his taxi a short distance away, and stood a half hour vigil with the Carleton Arms in plain view. The police cars remained, and as appeared to be the custom of the Vancouver police, a plainclothesman took up his position outside.

Finally, Jim went in search of another taxi, found one, had himself driven past the hotel where the trade commissioners from Turkey were staying, the Dunhill, did not notice much if any increased police activity there, and had his driver wait while he strolled into the tobacconist's establishment for a morning newspaper and another packet of cigarettes.

The spry little doorkeeper beamed on Hewlett. 'Well, all's quiet over there; nothing happened last night, and this morning when I opened the shop the detective out front came strolling from the dining-room as though he didn't have a thing on his mind.'

Hewlett pocketed the smokes, flipped open the newspaper, and slowly turned to gaze across the street. It was indeed quiet over there, and the police had reason to believe it would remain that way; they had *someone* on the run. They had the hotel where that *someone* had spent the night, staked out, with every reason to believe they'd nail Hewlett this morning. Additional guards at the Dunhill would seem superfluous, under those circumstances. Jim scanned the front page of his newspaper, winked at the older man and strolled back out to his taxi, and had himself driven to the airport.

Out there, in a place where orderly pandemonium, mingled with noise, made just one more human being seem unidentifiable, he sat in the parked taxi reading his newspaper, from time to time studying the beehive of activity visible through the immense glass windows. Whatever his hack-driver thought, seemed to be compensated for by the steadily ticking meter.

It took a full hour before Jim saw the cars

arrive, four of them, and each car had two plainclothesmen who alighted and moved like disciplined soldiers directly towards the front entrance of the terminal. Hewlett folded his newspaper, told the driver to head back for central Vancouver, and when the driver lit a cigarette, reminding Jim of the packet he'd recently purchased, he dug it out and left it lying upon the seat at his side.

Hollingsworth! Since he had tipped off the police, it was just as likely that he had tipped off the Turks. Why? Jim relaxed in the back of the cab. For as much money as he could get, no doubt, and while the police would pay him nothing, there was an excellent chance that Hamid Rumi *would.* A man with access to more money than most men could even count, and which only a very small handful of men could possibly earn in a lifetime, would certainly pay handsomely to get the information Hollingsworth had.

Jim suddenly jerked straight up on the seat. *Astarte!* If Hollingsworth had sold Jim out, then, for an additional fee—well up into the thousands, no doubt—he would also sell out Astarte to the man who had tried to murder her, and who would no doubt consider her unexpected survival the greatest possible threat to himself.

Jim paid off the hack in mid-town, sought a telephone where he would not be interrupted, and put in the long-distance call. Mary was at her desk when she answered.

'Good morning. Hewlett Special Services Agency. Miss Friday speaking,'

Jim spoke fast. 'Hewlett here. Friday, when did Hollingsworth call you?'

'How did you know that he called?'

'Friday, we can play games when I get home!'

'Sorry. He called last night, not very long after you'd called me.'

'At your flat?'

'Yes. I was as surprised as you are.'

'All right. Forget that for the time being. The telephone number he gave you for Astarte is traceable. You understand what I'm saying?'

'Yes, Mr Hewlett. But I'm mystified as to how you knew he gave me her number.'

'I'll explain later. I want you to trace that number to an address. Then I want you to go out there—use any excuse you can dream up—tell Astarte I told you to get her the hell out of that place, then find her a new hide-out. And Friday—*not* your apartment. Can you do this for me?'

'Certainly. You've just never given me the opportunity before. Mr Hewlett—is her life really in danger?'

'Yes. Hamid Rumi now knows she is alive. You can bet your boots, now that he has her fortune, he certainly has no intention of having her turn up alive. And Friday—not one word

96

of this to anyone at Benedict and Fleisher. Remember that, love, because once you stick your nose in this mess by hiding Astarte, that'll put you right up high on somebody's hit-list. *Not a word to anyone,* least of all to Hollingsworth, or anyone else at Benedict and Fleisher. Also—I didn't call you this morning. You haven't heard from me since last night. Clear?'

'Clear, Mr Hewlett.'

'Friday, if you bring it off, you can call me Jim, after this.'

'Oh, how wonderful, I've always wanted to call you—well, something.' Friday put down the telephone, leaving Hewlett standing there looking mildly surprised, as well as mildly suspicious. That was something else he'd have to take up with her, later.

Outside, the morning was passing, and unless he moved right along, so were his opportunities—which weren't very good, but at least they were better today than they had been yesterday.

The police now had three hotels staked out, the last one, plus the airport, being their best, from the standpoint of an apprehension.

That book on *bushido* had said that if an enemy were defensive, he would have to spread his men thin, while the redoubtable *samurai* could attack wherever his foe was weakest, relying upon the dauntless ferocity of his great sword, not to mention his

97

indomitable personal valour, as well as the overseeing, favourable providence of his ancestors.

Excluding the sword, the ancestors, and at least some of the indomitable valour, Jim Hewlett stood upon the kerbing gazing northward in the direction of the hotel, wondering whether Hamid Rumi would still be up there, and if so, whether whatever remained to Jim Hewlett of that indomitable valour, would sustain him now that he had decided to push hard for a confrontation. Probably not; in this kind of an affair valour could be a handicap, whereas infiltration, shrewdness, and deceit based entirely upon quick improvisation, helped like all hell.

There was no way for him to reach Rumi without a good bit of risk. The fact that the police were looking for him at the Carleton Arms, and when they decided he was not going to be trapped there, would then turn confidently to the airport, only meant that, for a very short while, perhaps no more than an hour and a half, they would not expect him to show up at the Dunhill.

But there would still be policemen in the building and around it.

There would also be the trade commissioners, if that is what they actually were. By now they would be alert, and perhaps a trifle jittery. It was impossible not to be a little jittery when it was known that a versatile

98

and experienced private agent was trying to break through the protective barriers. The Turks would undoubtedly be armed, now, if they hadn't been before. They would also have tightened their security, would have redoubled their precautions, would undoubtedly be staying close to one another.

Despite all this, in the light of what had happened so far, this morning was still the best of all times for Hewlett to make his attempt. The odds against success were formidable, but they were less so right now, and perhaps for the ensuing hour or so, than they would be this afternoon when the police discovered that Hewlett had never intended to appear at the airport, had instead, used that as a ruse.

He had the initiative, again. Not as he'd first had it, before Carl Hollingsworth had tried to get him either captured or killed, and in the interim, an entire screen of security had been thrown up against one man, James G. Hewlett.

He did not accept this as some kind of special inducement, some kind of test for his manliness or his professional expertise. He would have preferred to actually climb onto an airplane and return to Los Angeles, but, as with all the other principals in this affair, Hollingsworth, Rumi, and himself, there was all that money. There was also something else, with Hewlett—pride. Professionalism, and pride.

He went in search of a taxi which would

take him closer to the Dunhill, and during the ride he sat forward trying to imagine which ruse he would have to employ, after he had determined that Hamid Rumi was still at the hotel.

This was, actually, the hardest part of this kind of assignment. Improvisation was fine, with a violin, but when a man blew it with a violin, no one jumped up and shot him.

But there was no other way. Even improvisation offered damned few guarantees, when a cordon of police, bored or not, had to be overcome, deluded, penetrated somehow or other.

He left the cab, eventually, several squares southward, and on the same side of the street as the tobacconist's shop, strolled forward without any haste, gauging his progress to the stream of morning shoppers and business-people, who thronged the same sidewalk, in order to blend perfectly with this convenient human background, and kept watch for the plainclothesman over in front of the Dunhill.

The man was there, as usual, but Jim did not make that observation until he was only about half a square southward of the tobacconist's shop. There was just that one guard out front. If Astarte had been the secret informer, after Jim had fed her the information about making his attempt this morning, there would have been more than one policeman out there.

To be absolutely certain, though, he slackened gait just a little, and, working his way through the throng, got closer to the edge of the sidewalk. From there, he had an almost unimpeded opportunity to study the entire area over in front of the hotel.

There was still just that one plain-clothesman out front. Jim reached the intersection, fell in with the bustling morning flow of foot-traffic, got to the opposite side of the street, and hastened a little, again setting his gait to the people around him, who seemed to be mostly businessmen, and some women, on their way to offices in this particularly thriving part of Vancouver.

He passed within fifty yards of the guard out front of the Dunhill, saw the man's features clearly, and continued right on along, going eastward and beyond the view of the plainclothesman.

Chapter Eleven

Determining that the government car was still parked in its private area behind the hotel was easy. He entered the building which backed upon the same alleyway, and which happened to be a large department store, from the opposite square, searched out the men's lounge, and went into that private sanctum, which was fortunately otherwise unoccupied, lifted a rear-wall window and looked out.

The shiny government car being in place, meant that the trade commissioners had not left the hotel, yet.

Hewlett closed the window, left the men's room outward bound, hunted up a barber shop for a shave, and while relaxing under the hotel towel, reached his decision on how to proceed. It was not original; if there was an original way to affect this kind of penetration, it had yet to be revealed, but there were any number of methods which could be *tried*, and it was fair to assume that among all that number, there was one which could succeed. They had *all* succeeded at one time or another, someplace.

After the shave, he hunted up an inexpensive men's store, bought a large-size herringbone jacket, took it into the first available alley, kicked it back and forth upon the dirty pavement for a minute or two, then gathered it up, transferred some bank notes from his wallet to one pocket of the coat, put two of his business cards in the opposite pocket, then walked briskly back in the direction of the Dunhill.

But he did not approach the plainclothesman out front, instead, he halted where a uniformed officer was standing upon the kerbing at the nearby intersection, evidently a traffic officer, and said, 'I just saw a man, or maybe it was two men, in the alleyway back along the east side of the street, but across the road, drop this jacket. It was hard to see into the alley, and anyway, I was striding past and only glanced in. By the time I turned back for a second look, there was no one in the alley, but this coat was lying where they'd been struggling —if there were two of them, which I couldn't be sure of.'

The uniformed officer accepted the coat, glanced briefly at Jim, then pulled something from a pocket of the herringbone jacket. It was some crumpled money. The uniformed officer straightened up looking down where the plainclothesman was standing, and hesitated, then he reached inside his tunic for a pen and a small book. 'Your name?' he asked. Jim replied instantly and blandly. 'Ralph Maginnis.' He also gave an address. Then he said, 'This is going to make me even later at the office.' He raised an arm to point. 'I'm with Columbian Insurance, on the sixth floor of that building.' He started edging away even before the uniformed man nodded, then turned and briskly walked down where the plainclothesman was standing.

Jim fell in with the surging tide of pedestrians, remained on the far side next to the kerbing while watching the detective accept, and begin examining, the herringbone jacket, and as he and the uniformed man spoke back and forth while the detective looked at the crumpled notes, then felt in the other pockets, Jim angled across through the crowd, entered the Dunhill by its ornate, heavy doors, and strolled across the lobby to the lift, where he purchased a newspaper by dropping a coin into a small metal container and lifting a steel bale to take out the paper. He punched a lift button, opened the paper, folded it halfway, and watched the front doors. No one entered until just before the automatic lift arrived, and then it was not the plainclothesman, it was a heavy woman in her middle years wearing a very expensive pearl-grey fur coat, despite the outside temperature, which had to be well up into the hot seventies.

The lift was empty. He rode it up one more flight than was necessary, went down an empty, carpeted corridor to the farthest window along the back of the building, looked out, saw the attached steel fire-escape out there, and also saw a solitary man strolling in the direction of the government car. He stood and watched while the man in the parking area bent a little, unlocked the door on the driver's side of the government vehicle, rolled down a window, then with no show of haste at all, leaned upon the car while he lighted a cigarette.

Jim drew back, returned to the row of lifts, selected an empty one and rode to the ninth floor. He met the first person he'd seen since embarking from the lobby, on the ninth floor. A jowelly elderly man with great tufted eyebrows and a pair of keen, slightly glowering eyes. They nodded as the jowelly man entered the lift Jim had just vacated, the door slowly closed, and the last Hewlett saw of the jowelly old man, was his right hand; there was a massive gold ring on one thick finger showing a large, icy-bright diamond in the centre of a Masonic emblem. Then the door closed, the little light came on overhead, and the lift began a slow descent.

Jim went along to the abrupt turn of this upper, carpeted corridor, and nearly collided with a thin, tall woman whose flashing very dark eyes made an almost startling contrast to her pale skin and frosted, silvery hair. She still had the key of her suite dangling from her hand. The numbered tag attached to the key swung between the dark-eyed woman's fingers. She smiled at Jim, her only reaction to their near-collision as each had rounded the corner, then she passed from sight in the direction of the lifts, and Jim moved down the corridor in the direction she had come, came to the correct door, fished out his own keyring, and, using a small, hooked implement upon it, opened the door of the room whose number corresponded with the number on the key-tag of the dark-eyed woman.

Inside, the place smelled faintly of some kind of flower, gardenia or perhaps honeysuckle. From that, plus one or two other observations, Jim decided that the dark-eyed woman was a widow, which was the extent of his immediate interest in her. He went to the telephone, lifted it, laid it upon its stand, jangled the dial, then loudly said, 'Damn it, be careful, can't you? You want everyone in the place swarming up here before we're finished? Hey, I think I found her valuables. Over here. Come have a look.'

He imitated a second man, somewhat disgruntled, swore a good bit, then leaned down listening for any change in the dial-tone. It came, ultimately, just a small, solitary crackling sound as though someone had broken the connection. That was the sound he'd wanted to hear.

He left the room, hurried along to the lift, rode down to the fifth floor, alighted, and used the stairs, making his approach to the floor of the Turkish trade commission quietly and unobtrusively. He saw the plainclothesman near the lifts, standing over there doing something with the hand-set of his transceiver unit. The corridor was lighted at intervals along its full length, and excepting the plainclothesman, it was empty, at least for the few moments immediately following Jim Hewlett's descent of the stairs, almost to the corridor, where he hung back, eyeing the detective, but moments later a man and a woman emerged from one of the rooms midway along, bringing the bored detective's interest around, and away from his radio. The couple were well-dressed and fairly youthful. They were dressed for the street, the man had a leather camera-case in one hand, and the woman, who led the way to the lift, was carrying a case for sunglasses. As they passed the detective the man smiled and muttered something. Jim did not hear the words, but he distinctly heard the answer:

'Yes, it's tiresome, but it'll be ending soon, I think.'

The detective smiled, the couple stood at the lift, and when it arrived they entered, and disappeared. The detective glanced around, stepped closer to one of the overhead lights and raised the transceiver again. Jim moved, now, approaching as swiftly as he dared over the heavy, sound-deadening carpet. The detective did not hear him, could not have heard him since he made no noise at all, but at the very last moment, the detective started to turn, perhaps functioning on instinct. Jim had both arms raised and in position. He caught hold of the detective with his left arm by sliding it beneath the man's arms from behind, above the elbows, and pinioning the detective. His right hand encircled the man's throat, temporarily cutting off the man's breath. He swung him against the wall, growled him into a face-forward motionless stance, then raised both hands, pressed lightly behind the man's ears, lower, on his neck, and the detective fell, unconscious.

Jim dragged him to the curve of the corridor, left him there, and moved swiftly, with the man's transceiver in his hand, to the door where the detective had been standing, raised a hand and knocked twice, lightly.

He was holding the police transceiver to his face when the Turk opened the door. Over the Turk's shoulder another man was visible, holding a cup of coffee in his hands, facing half around, away from the door. Hamid Rumi. Jim knew him at once. He started to lower the transceiver as though to speak, using his left hand, and without warning caught the man in front of him flush on the point of the jaw, with his right fist. The Turk went over backwards as though he were a half-sack of wet meal. He did not even roll, when he came down upon the carpet. Jim had one glance of the man with the coffee cup, turning, his rather handsome, pale face, mirroring complete astonishment.

Jim stepped over the knocked-out man and crossed towards Rumi in three big strides. He had thought Rumi had been speaking to someone beyond his range of sight, when he'd had his first glimpse of the interior of the suite, but when he got over there, only Rumi was visible. But there was a closed door in the south wall, in the direction Hamid Rumi had been looking, so perhaps there *had* been another man, and he had just gone into the adjoining room.

Hewlett said, 'Keep your hands where I can see them. Put the cup down and let's move.'

The astonished Turk stood and stared. Finally, he said, 'You're J. G. Hewlett?'

Jim reached, took the cup, put it aside and pointed to the door. 'No, I'm the tooth-fairy. *Move!*' He gave the slightly shorter and only half as wide man a light, rough shove. As Rumi went past, Jim ran both hands up and down him in a quick, experienced frisk. The man had an automatic. Jim halted him at the door, plucked out the gun and pitched it backwards upon a sofa. 'To the stairs,' he ordered.

Rumi said, 'You'll never make it, Hewlett. They've known about you for several days. They have a cordon of police around the hotel. No one comes in, or goes out, without—'

'Move! And shut up!' He herded his prisoner towards the stairs. Just before he pointed downward, he said. 'Any time you can get *into* a guarded place, Rumi, you can get *out.* All you need is luck.'

They descended slowly. Once, when the transceiver bleeped, they halted while Jim listened to an exchange between policemen on the ninth floor, and someone in position elsewhere, presumably in or near the lobby. The upstairs men reported that there were no burglars in Mrs Evans's room, and it did not appear as though the suite had been ransacked. Jim did not wait, he shoved Rumi and continued on his way.

They left the main stairwell where a steel-lined, fire-proof door opened upon another set of stairs, this time of steel and cement, without carpeting and not as adequately lighted. These steps continued downward as far as the lobby-level, where there was another of those fireproof doors, this service door was at the lobby-level. They turned on the landing and continued their descent. Hamid Rumi turned once, to look enquiringly at Jim Hewlett. Then, without a word, he went along.

The labyrinth beneath the hotel was chilly, lighted by bulbs encased in small steel cages, and seemed to be well-used. There were storerooms, with red-painted numerals on their doors, the corridors and rooms were very neat and clean, and the huge boiler-room shone with the brightness of a constant care. This particular room, with its brass, copper, insulated pipes and steel gratings, reminded Hewlett of the engine room of a naval vessel.

Here, finally, Hamid Rumi halted and turned to speak. 'Mr Hewlett, there is no way out—except one way.' His English was very good, with a faint trace of accent. 'You are a businessman. So am I.'

Jim, using this moment to determine which of the subterranean corridors led towards the rear of the building, answered disinterestedly. 'Save your breath—and your offer of a bribe. Turn right, up there, beyond the insulated tanks, and keep walking.'

'. . . Fifty thousand US dollars, Mr Hewlett?'

Jim's eyes dropped to the handsome, deceptively mild-looking face. 'Turn right at the tanks.' They looked at one another for a moment, then the Turk turned, and did as he had been told. He did not make another attempt to speak until they were on a slight cement ramp leading upwards towards a very large, wide, fireproof steel door, obviously, the way out of the basement, and, Jim hoped into the alleyway. Then Rumi said, 'In case you hadn't heard, Mr Hewlett, they even have the FBI waiting at all border check-points out of Canada. You're just not going to be able to bring this off. And even if you could—the laws in your country for kidnapping are—'

'Shut up, will you?' growled Jim, eyeing the big door.

Chapter Twelve

The big steel-lined alleyway door yielded easily from the inside. From the outside, there was no way to make it open, unless one had the proper key.

Jim shoved Rumi to the edge of the door-jamb and held him there with one hand while he looked out. The alleyway seemed to be empty. He stepped ahead a foot and glanced over where he'd seen the man near the government car. Neither the man nor the car were in the parking area.

He pulled the Turk outside with him, did not say a word as he hustled his captive directly across the alley to the back of the department-store building, where the open window was, told Rumi to climb upwards, and before the Turk's legs had disappeared into the men's room, Jim was crowding in through the window too.

Again, fortunately, the rest-room, was unoccupied.

This was the stroke of luck he had referred to, back in the Dunhill. Hamid Rumi, adjusting his jacket, looked at big Jim Hewlett, and almost smiled. Then he wagged his head as though in grudging respect, and awaited whatever came next.

It was a very short wait. Jim opened the

door leading out into the crowded store, and jerked his head for Rumi to precede him. As the Turk walked forth he said, 'You look a little conspicuous, with that walkie-talkie in your coat pocket.'

They mingled with the throng of bargain-hunters, working their way towards the front of the store. Rumi offered no resistance at any point, although it must have crossed his mind that, in the crowded store, he could probably have escaped, or at least, if he started a commotion, Hewlett would have to flee in order to avoid being captured. Perhaps the Turk's respect of his hulking companion was influenced by a suspicion that Hewlett was armed—which he was not—and might use a gun.

They left the department-store, stepped into the brilliant sunshine, and when Rumi looked up, quizzically, Jim turned him southward among the throng of pedestrians, and remained close as they strode along.

By now, the detective who'd succumbed to the old judo trick of rendering a man unconscious by depriving his brain of blood, and oxygen, at the correct pressure points, had regained consciousness. The Turk who had had the misfortune to run head-on into Hewlett's fist, would also be recovering, but much more slowly, and no doubt, if Jim dared raise the transceiver to listen, he would hear excited and chagrined voices snapping orders back and forth.

From this juncture on, it was going to be a race and a manhunt, with nearly all the advantages on the side of the manhunters. But there was one slim chance; Jim understood the strategy of this one slim chance as well as the police did. Keep moving. Don't stop, regardless of how safe, or how tired, one got. Hunters only succeeded when the pursued paused, or halted, or got too confident and stopped running. If the police were able to arrive at the places where Hewlett *had been,* without glimpsing their prey, they would remain the hunters and Hewlett would remain free. Now, he had to rely upon his previous, careful orientation of the city, as well as movement.

They caught a taxi and rode two miles, in the direction of the conference building, but on an oblique angle which took them to a part of Vancouver where the sea-scent was stronger, and where the industry appeared to be sea-oriented. There were freezing plants, canning establishments, and large complexes for storage. Here, the people were more roughly attired. Here, the weather was cooler, and in fact remained cooler all summer, and also remained correspondingly warmer in winter because of its proximity to the Strait.

Hamid Rumi relaxed in the cab. When they left it, and resumed their odyssey on foot, he adopted an attitude of philosophical resignation, not entirely devoid of interest. Obviously, Jim Hewlett was not going to harm him; at least, Hewlett had not come intentionally to harm him, or he wouldn't have brought him this far. If he'd been hired for an assassination, he would have left Rumi dead on the floor of the suite at the Dunhill.

As they walked, now, through the busy, noisy, smelly area of the city, Rumi tried to start up conversation. He said, 'I don't imagine how you can bring this off. Not in this city, and not at the border. I think your only course is to accept my offer. Even then, it's doubtful that you can return to your country.'

Hewlett looked at the slighter, lean and muscular man. Hamid Rumi smiled. He had a pleasant smile. It was hard to equate what Jim saw, with what he knew, of this man. But Hamid Rumi certainly was not the first deadly human being to appear as anything but what he really was.

When Jim said nothing, Rumi went on speaking. 'I know who hired you. I know all about you, The Vancouver police are very efficient. They gave me a report about you, Mr Hewlett. I was impressed. I'm still impressed, but after all, having been educated at Harvard, in the US, I know very well that the US has men as resourceful as you are. I also know that private investigators in the US don't make a lot of money. Fifty thousand dollars and my co-operation in helping you escape, ought to mean something to you.'

Jim's reply was dry. 'Fifty thousand here, fifty thousand there. You could go on like that for the rest of your life, and still not make much of a dent in a hundred million dollars.'

Hamid Rumi's nostrils flared and his black gaze narrowed slightly. 'Do you favour the opium trade, Mr Hewlett? I don't think you do. Not very many Americans favour it. Well; that's where her father made it, in the opium trade.'

Jim smiled humourlesly at Hamid Rumi, the man who had been a secret assassin for Turkey's opium interests, and who was now pretending that the interests he had served, and for all Jim knew, was still serving, were contemptible. Instead of prolonging this discussion, he pointed to a small, dilapidated shed near the waterfront. 'We'll wait in there until nightfall,' he said.

Rumi looked at the abandoned shed, looked beyond, where a grimy inlet surged with the sluggish run of the daytime tide, then shook his head. 'By sea,' he said, 'Of course. But you still won't make it.' As they left the pavement stepping through the desolate, uninspiring litter towards the shack, he made another comment. 'People talk. The man who'll run the boat will talk. We are leaving a trail the police won't have much trouble following, you know. Even the cab-driver, back there, will remember us.' He paused just outside the

116

broken door of the shack. 'They'll be swarming over the city right this minute. If we sit in here until evening—'

'You sure talk a lot,' grunted Jim, shoving the Turk through the door into the dirty, gloomy interior of the old shed.

Rumi turned. 'What else do we do, but talk? Now, you have stopped moving. Now, we will wait until evening—but the police aren't waiting.'

Jim looked sharply at his prisoner. Rumi also understood the strategy of pursuit, or he wouldn't have emphasised the fact that they would await nightfall—which was not what Jim was doing at all— even though Rumi obviously thought he was.

'We're going to have a little discussion, here,' he told his prisoner. 'We're going to discuss the means by which you will transfer your wife's fortune back to her.' Jim shoved fisted hands into his pockets, facing the Turk.

Rumi made a small gesture with his hands. 'Do you imagine I have it with me, on my person?'

'No. By now you've put it in a safe place, a Canadian bank, but you're the key to it, aren't you? So—we're going to work out the method to be used in transferring it to her, down in California. And Rumi, despite what Carl Hollingsworth told you, she's not there. She's not where Hollingsworth's law firm hid her.'

The Turk showed nothing, but evidently

Hewlett had made a good point, because Hamid Rumi stared at him for a moment, before speaking again. Then all he said, was: 'Not *fifty* thousand dollars, Mr Hewlett, seventy-five thousand dollars. You're more than just a strong-arm man, evidently. All right; seventy-five thousand dollars, and you'll work for me.'

'I'm not for sale, like Hollingsworth, Rumi, but even if I was, you couldn't afford me,' stated Hewlett.

'One hundred thousand dollars, Hewlett.'

Jim smiled. 'You've got that in your wallet?'

'No, of course not, but—'

'There are no "buts". Getting back to the hundred million you're going to return to your wife . . .'

The Turk stared stonily at Hewlett. 'Never, in this world.'

Jim continued to smile. 'You're wrong about that. You're going to do it—because a hundred million, or ten times that much, isn't worth a damn to a dead man.'

'You're not a killer, Hewlett. I know what kind of a man you are. You're not a—'

'You just made a very bad assessment of character, Rumi, and in this kind of a game, you don't get any second chances. I can kill you with my hands. What makes you think your wife wouldn't have you killed? She's got a hell of a scar where you made your attempt. The difference is, I won't fail.'

118

They stood in the filth and squalor of the abandoned shack facing each other. Beyond, there were the muted sounds of a busy shoreline during a work-day at the peak of its season. Occasionally, a whistle shrilled. It could have been ashore, among the fish canneries, or it could have been a signal to the shore one of the busy trawlers sent ahead to serve notice that a hold full of fish was approaching.

It was also a totally unreal background for the discussion between the two men in the old shed. The people of this section of Vancouver worked hard, in unskilled or semi-skilled capacities, they could not even *dream* in the sums of money the two men in the shack were discussing.

Hamid Rumi fished forth a packet of cigarettes and lit one. Then, as he exhaled smoke, gazing at his captor, he said, 'She didn't hire you to kill me. But it wouldn't make much difference in your case, anyway. You're in more trouble than you'll ever again be in, in your life. I mean it when I say there's only one way out for you. I've had this in mind since they told me someone was trying to reach me, and later, when they had identified you as J. G. Hewlett, the private investigator from California, I didn't worry, because whether you failed or succeeded, I still held the whiphand.' Rumi inhaled, considered the glowing tip of his cigarette, and said, 'You're not a fool at all,

Mr Hewlett. You're a clever man.' The black eyes swept up. 'I read all about you . . . I'm not just thinking of this particular affair. I'm thinking of my expanding interests in Canada, and later in the US. Mr Hewlett, the hardest of all commodities to buy is something you have, and something I need very much—loyalty.'

Jim listened, then slowly wagged his head. 'You're off the damned track again. You're going to give her back her fortune.'

Rumi shook his head. 'I am *not* going to give her back her fortune.'

'Can you swim—with your arms tied behind you?'

Instead of answering the question, the Turk's eyes narrowed a little. After a thoughtful moment he said, 'I understand. She has offered you more, but contingent upon her getting the fortune back. Isn't that it?'

Jim shook his head. '*She* isn't paying me at all. In fact, believe it or not, I've only seen her once, and don't even know what her full name is.'

Rumi scowled. 'Benedict and Fleisher, then?'

'That's correct. Benedict and Fleisher. And when I get back, I'm going to break Hollingsworth's neck.'

Rumi shrugged. 'That doesn't concern me.'

'How much did you promise him?'

'Promise him? Mr Hewlett, I *paid* him. I didn't promise him. Fifteen thousand dollars.'

Rumi dropped the cigarette and stepped on it. 'He came cheap, didn't he?'

'Not for what you got, Mr Rumi, because you can't find *her,* and as long as she's alive, you're in trouble up to your neck. Now listen to me; we're going out in a boat shortly, and whether you ever reach land again is going to depend upon what you agree to.' Jim studied the handsome, deceptive features of Hamid Rumi briefly, then spoke on. 'If you're sincere about not yielding, then you're going to make an unpleasant discovery. You don't think I'll kill you? Wait and see.'

In the near distance a trawler let go a blast with a klaxon horn that carried inland a considerable distance. Nearby, someone answered with two short blasts on a less strident whistle.

Elsewhere, gulls cried, and the steady, lesser sound of steam escaping from a stack made a steady, strong hissing.

Chapter Thirteen

Hewlett listened to the transceiver, discovered that the conversations he was picking up were almost entirely in some kind of code, decided that the police knew he had the transceiver, pocketed it, and took his captive on a stroll up the shoreline, during the course of which Rumi said, 'I'll make a compromise with you, Hewlett. I'll give instructions at the Vancouver bank for all the interest which will accrue on the money to go to my wife, for one year. Have you any idea how much that is? She can live very comfortably for the rest of her life on that much money.'

Jim, eyeing the small boats riding in the shallows that they strolled past, turned an ironic gaze upon the Turk. 'How long would she live? A year, six months?'

'All right. I'll give you my word—'

'Your word isn't worth anything, Rumi. You've read all about me, well, I happen to have dug up a little about you as well, and now that I've met you, I can see how you'd be so successful at your trade. You don't look the part. It must have been a hell of a shock to some of the people you went out to get, to be killed by a man who looked like a schoolteacher.'

They halted near an old whaleboat with a

high pitch to its stem and stern. It had been modified for a small inboard motor, too small, actually for sea-going trips, but quite adequate for inlet fishing. Jim leaned on the beached bow, shaking his head. 'You're making this hard for both of us. Maybe it hasn't soaked in yet, but as I said before, what good is a hundred million dollars to a dead man? That's your choice. For all I know, she might even give you a little of her money, if you return it.' Jim shrugged thick shoulders. 'But the fortune is going back to her, one way or another.'

'What—one way or another?'

'She's your wife. If you turn up dead, she's also your heir. It worked for you, when everyone thought she was dead, didn't it? Well, then it ought to work in reverse.' Jim cast a long glance at the diminishing signs of this long day, over against the rugged skyline, before saying, 'If you think *I'm* in trouble, start thinking about yourself.' He straightened up, glanced both ways along the deserted stretch of beach, then said, 'Give me a hand.'

Hamid Rumi turned slowly and stared at the old whaleboat. 'This is yours?' he asked.

Jim's reply was made while he leaned to ease the craft back into a rising tide. 'No, it's not mine. I never saw it before. But we'll borrow it. Now lean and lend a hand.'

Rumi gazed enquiringly at Hewlett, briefly, then leaned. They had no difficulty getting the old boat into the tide. Rumi jumped in, stood wide-legged gazing at the inboard motor, then went past to the stern and sat down to watch Jim Hewlett.

The boat, itself, for all its advanced age, was seaworthy, and under the impetus of twelve powerful oarsmen would have been able to survive in a moderately rough sea, but the inboard motor someone had painstakingly installed in it, was one-third the size and horsepower it should have been, just to handle a craft this size, let alone to handle such a craft with two passengers aboard, unless of course it was not asked to do more than navigate the inland strait.

Jim surprised himself when he sank down beside the little motor to coax it to life. The motor started with his first try. He motioned Rumi for'ard, set the heavy old wooden tiller in place, swung the bow, and headed slightly southwesterly, on a diagonal run across the inlet. Rumi lit another cigarette, alternately watching the shoreline, and Jim Hewlett. It would not have taken him long to discover that his captor was an experienced small-boat-man.

To reach Vancouver Island from the city across the inlet, two able men in a whaleboat did not even need that small motor, they could have rowed the entire distance—except that there were no oars in the whaleboat, only one over-sized paddle, and it was secured to one side below the gun'nals by metal clips, evidently for use only in emergencies.

The motor ran perfectly . . . Evidently, like the boat, that little motor had received a lot of care from someone to whom both the boat and its power plant, were quite special.

There appeared to be a low fog across the inlet, over against the inland shoreline, something to be expected in wintertime, perhaps, but not to be expected, at least not very often, in summertime. When they were close enough to hear the surf breaking, Hamid Rumi stood up and listened, then he called to Jim.

'Do you know this shoreline?'

Jim smiled back. 'I've never been anywhere near any of this country in my life. Why?'

'Because I can hear the sea smashing against rocks, through the fog.'

Jim cocked his head, heard nothing he thought was broken surf, and smiled back at the Turk. 'Can you swim?'

Rumi scowled. 'If you try to go in, where that fog stands, you'll run into those damned rocks.'

They did not go in. That had not been Jim's intention from the time he first set his course. There was an area, if they could reach it, directly across from the city-proper, where a series of visible reefs created an irregular extrusion of land. He had seen them for the first time from the air, when he had arrived in Vancouver. He had in mind threading these inlets, and the closer the whaleboat got to that

125

area, the more traffic was encountered.

Beyond those islands lay the curving coastline of the most populous segment of the entire area. Nor were all the vessels which came inland from that locale, rounding the Cape Flattery headland, fishing trawlers. There were also a number of stately excursion vessels large enough to be completely seaworthy. But by and far, the majority of craft were either deep-water trawlers, or shallow-water fishing boats no larger, or at least not *much* larger, than the whaleboat.

They ran out of fog before coming down the inlet-side of Vancouver Island, to the broken, irregular islets at the island's southerly tip, but in its place was an unusually heavy traffic of boats. Evidently fishing was being very productive around the tip of Vancouver Island, and out the strait into the choppy sea. Also, no doubt because this was the holidaying time of year, those huge excursion vessels seemed to be running in packs.

For Hamid Rumi, all this had to be an eye-opener, but for Jim Hewlett, who was anything but a novice with small-craft, the constant changes of course he was called upon to make, as they made their way steadily towards the southward tip of the island, were a welcome challenge. It called upon his best seamanship, and it also, at least for a short time, allowed him to forget the unpleasant business that was keeping him in the northwest.

Once, some kind of government vessel, not much larger than their whaleboat, shot from between two large fishing trawlers, and Jim had to lean hard on his rudder. As the government boat sped past, its helmsman raised a hand in a high salute. Jim waved back, and kept an eye on the patrol vessel, but it kept to its forward course. Rumi, watching from a seat amidships, said, 'You're lucky. They must have recognised the boat.'

That was quite possible. Of course, if the patrol craft had come closer, had *not* recognised the pair of strangers manning the boat, whose owner they probably knew, then it would have been a different story,

Rumi pointed and yelled. 'That's black water! Mind the rocks and the shallows!'

Hewlett, already angling to avoid the shallows near a desolate shelf of partially submerged rock whose upper segment was a narrow, fairly long, island, called back. 'Where did you sail?'

'In the Mediterranean,' retorted the Turk, leaning to watch as the submerged rock glided clear on their starboard side. As he straightened up, he yanked off his tie, stuffed it into a jacket pocket, removed the jacket and dropped it athwart his seat in the middle of the boat.

Jim laughed. Evidently the Turk thought he was going to have to swim for it, yet.

Finally, they found a deep-water passage

among the little nuisance-islands. The way they found it in all that boat- and ship-traffic, was by watching the dignified, and ponderous, passageway a pair of large ships took on their outward-bound course. At once, the wind stiffened a little, and the sea-scent was much stronger.

Rumi scowled. 'You can't run into the sea in this thing. Look, it's choppy, and we aren't even beyond land yet.'

Hewlett pretended to ponder this admonition. Eventually he smiled at the Turk. 'We're not going to sea. We don't have to.' He pointed. 'We're going across the inlet towards that distant headland.'

The bight was much wider than it appeared on the map Jim had studied so painstakingly the afternoon of his first arrival in British Columbia. In fact, as they swung half-about, being compelled to broach the tide, their vessel was repeatedly struck broadsides by choppy little forceful waves.

Hamid Rumi looked around, looked back, then shook his head with an exaggerated expression of disgust. Finally, immediately after a particularly hard wave had struck the old whaleboat, he said, 'You were right. You damned well may drown me. But it'll be because you're a poor sailor, not an assassin.'

Jim laughed, held to his course, and only when their little motor spluttered, did he take his eyes off a bit of land he was using to hold his course by, since they had no compass.

Hamid Rumi leaned over the motor, up-ended a small red can, worked professionally for a few moments under Jim's interested gaze, and the little motor resumed its busy little cadence again. Rumi, wiping both hands on his trousers, looked up and said, 'Needed fuel.'

Jim smiled. 'Thanks.'

The Turk gave him a black-eyed, long look, then shook his head again.

The day was nearing its end, there was more than just a chill blowing up the strait from the yonder sea, there was also a clammy, vague mistiness which would probably turn into a full fog after sundown.

Jim had already considered this, and its relationship to that far headland they were making for, but Hamid Rumi's head suddenly came up and around, facing the direction of the distant sea. For a moment he sat like that, before turning in the opposite direction, towards the craggy destination along the far coastline, which seemed to be quite a few miles below what appeared to be a quite large city. Rumi then said, 'We're not going to make it, that far down the coast. You'd better change course to bring us in closer to that city.'

Jim said, 'We'll make it,' and did not change the slant of his tiller one iota.

The chill increased, Rumi put his jacket back on, and the running tide brisked up as the wind created small white-caps. The old whaleboat yielded to the force of the tide with an almost fatalistic acceptance, almost as though it possessed a mind—and knowledge— of its own. They were being pushed towards that big city where immense smoke-stacks belched plumes of smoke into the fading brilliance of the ending day, but the more they were forced to yield, the harder Jim manned his tiller so that their course was rather like that of a drunken man, being compelled in one direction, while simultaneously refusing with stubborn tenacity, to yield in his onward course. Rumi, watching, estimating their ultimate destination, and seeing a fresh string of islands looming ahead, to stand between their whaleboat and the farther mainland, threw up his hands, but he said nothing, until, when they were closer to the protection of the land, the wind and tide let up a little, and their boat stood a little straighter on its keel-less bottom, then he said, 'You're going to make it.'

Jim grinned. 'Did you doubt it?'

The Turk's black eyes lifted, full of hard irony. 'No one but a damned fool would *not* have doubted it.'

They swung beyond the first island, and found themselves in a literal maze of other, smaller islands, still with the densely populated shoreline in their port side. Jim eyed the fading sky, studied the landforms, and finally turned up between two wild and wooded small islands to make a straight run towards the beach. Rumi guessed his purpose and gripped the gun'nals. When the whaleboat reached the shallows, it ploughed ahead, rose once on a gentle surf, and came down, also gently, hard aground in the sucking sand.

Jim jumped out, hauling the anchor-line with him, went briskly to a large tree, made his bowline, then watched the Turk step gingerly ahead in the craft, until he was at the bow, then jump. He almost reached hard ground, but not quite, and as his shoes sank to his ankles in mud and water, he cursed. Jim laughed.

'Welcome to the US,' he said.

Hamid Rumi, standing in sandy muck, looked up, then looked around. 'I don't believe it.'

Jim kept smiling. 'Come along, we've got some walking to do before dark . . . You can believe it.'

Rumi dragged a foot at a time from the muck, and trudged forward.

Chapter Fourteen

The countryside was rough, overgrown, and well-populated. The farther from the shoreline they walked, the more small farms they encountered, along with a network of paved roads. By late dusk, when they halted so that the abducted Turk could remove his shoes and rid them of as much sand as he could shake loose, they were in what appeared to be an area of great lumber mills, interspersed among small landholdings. When Rumi had his shoes on and stood up, looked at Jim Hewlett as though there were something bothering him, and said, 'You didn't plan this, did you? I mean, you aren't following some preconceived plan.'

'I told you, I've never been up here before in my life, which means I have no contacts up here, so how could I make plans?'

The Turk said, 'You're crazy,' and trudged along beside Hewlett. 'You're either crazy, or you've got more confidence than anyone I've ever known.'

They found a clearing where men had recently felled all the merchantable timber for many acres in all directions. There was a rutted, soggy road leading from this timberlanding, southwestward. As they crossed the clearing and reached the road, Jim

Hewlett said, 'How well do you remember US geography?'

The Turk did not answer. 'Why?'

'Because this is the state of Washington. Below Washington is the state of Oregon, and below Oregon is California. We're not too far from where we're going.'

Hamid Rumi looked around with a baffled expression; 'You think we can *walk* to California?'

'No. But I think we're going to walk until we find a secluded, wooded spot, and from there, I'll go on alone.'

Rumi didn't believe the implication. 'Why didn't you shoot me back at the hotel, then?'

'Too noisy, too many police around.'

'Then—why not in the boat?'

Hewlett sighed. 'All right; you and I *aren't* alike. I'm *not* an assassin.'

Rumi halted in his tracks. 'Then what's the purpose of all this? Even if you can get me all the way to California, you're not going to win. I'm not going to give back the money.'

Jim smiled. 'Care to bet on that?'

Rumi's baffled expression returned. 'How . . . ?'

Jim pointed along the rutted road, and without speaking they trudged along. For a mile the road, which had evidently been bladed out by a large tractor for the exclusive use of large timber-trucks, meandered through scrub undergrowth amid bristly stands of

133

second- third -and fourth-growth pines. The road suddenly swung abruptly to the left, climbed a short incline, and intersected a wide, paved throughway. Cars were infrequent along through here. Their headlamps gave a forewarning of their approach for a full mile before they passed.

Jim studied the terrain, as best he could in the settling night, then gestured on across the throughway where another of those logging-roads went out through more rough, somewhat overgrown and mountainous country. Hamid Rumi shook his head. 'No more walking,' he exclaimed. 'You don't know where you're going. You don't even know where you *are.*'

That was true, but Jim gave the Turk a rough push and they crossed the pavement to the next logging-road, and with their backs to the paved road, went trudging onward again. A car passed, behind them, its lights casting an oblique dull brilliance around them. Jim said nothing, but kept walking, only growling now and then when his companion dragged behind a little.

The night wore along. It was not as cold as it was damp and clammy. Once, when Rumi said they should stop, at least until daybreak, Jim kept him going, saying only that they had a lot of country to cross before daylight.

The Turk walked, buttoned his jacket, and finally, shortly before midnight, he turned up his collar, shoved both hands into trouser pockets, and hunched along with his tired body slightly bent at the shoulders. Jim did not let up. He had not let up all day, and now he did not let up all night.

The raw sea-scent eventually faded, to be replaced with an equally as raw a scent of damp earth, and mould. It obviously rained a lot in this particular area; ferns, creepers, small trees, and many varieties of hardy, flourishing, man-high bushes and weeds abounded. When they ran out of one rough logging-road, they quartered until they found another one, and kept hiking along.

By three o'clock in the morning, when the dampness and the clammy chill was almost noticeable, Hamid Rumi stopped and glared. 'This is insane. We're not getting anywhere. I've got a blister on my heel.' He started to ease down beside the muddy road, but Jim caught him by one arm and kept him standing.

'Walk,' he told the Turk. 'And keep walking.'

Rumi put a rebellious, puzzled look upon Hewlett. 'Where?' he demanded. 'You are absolutely crazy. We can't possibly walk all the way to—'

'Save your breath,' said Jim, and shoved the Turk ahead of him, on down the faintly star-lighted rough roadway.

They did not stop again, nor speak to one another, until shortly before daybreak, when the Turk, obviously travelling on stamina alone, by this time, halted beside a tree and leaned there.

Ahead, downward and across a wide swale which had been cleared for farms, was a village. In the unreal light of false-dawn, it looked dead or deserted. There was only one light shining, and that seemed to be above a log structure in the centre of the village, where someone had neglected to take down the flag the evening before.

Rumi could see the flag well enough to identify it, which seemed to confirm a vague doubt he'd entertained that they were, actually, across the international boundary line.

Gazing down at that little sleeping village, he said, 'I know what you're trying to do, Hewlett. You're trying to wear me down.' He turned, only his head, and continued to lean. 'I'm not going another step.'

Jim's answer was quiet. 'Care to bet on it? You're going to keep moving, if I have to kick your britches and keep you in front of me to do it.'

Rumi did not move. 'All right. I'll make you a proposition. I'll give you fifty thousand dollars just to walk on by yourself.'

Jim looked disgusted. 'You've already made that offer a couple of times. And you don't have *fifty* dollars, let alone fifty thousand dollars.'

'I have it,' stated the Turk. 'In Canada I deposited—'

'That's in Canada. We're in the state of Washington. Now push off that damned tree and *walk!*'

They moved out again, avoided the village without much trouble, crossed another paved road, paralleled it for a hundred or so yards, until Jim saw another pair of meandering ruts, and this time, as they hiked along, the country began to become increasingly hilly, and overgrown.

Dawn arrived, the sun came—and an hour later great soiled clouds covered the sun, and a heavy drizzle began. Hamid Rumi tried to light a cigarette for breakfast, and the rain put it out. He cursed, and turned on Jim, who raised a warning hand.

'Walk!'

They kept on trudging, both of them in suits, in city shoes, looking ludicrous in the wilds of up-state Washington.

The drizzle continued until almost ten o'clock, then those soiled old clouds drifted away northward, the sun came out, and steam arose. The heat was bad; it would not have been so bad if the humidity, and the soaked ground, did not respond to it by making the stillness and the humidity blend with the dripping undergrowth, to make walking hard and breathing even harder.

Hamid Rumi's voice roughened. He was hungry, he said. Jim did not relent, nor did he go anywhere close to the small villages they saw, from time to time. Once, as they pressed along a brushy ridge overlooking a large lake—which was actually a mill pond—they saw a huge lumber mill. The noise, even from a mile distant, was loud.

From this point on, as the land turned into a series of broken, up-ended, overgrown hills, rocky underfoot and steaming with moist heat, Hamid Rumi's strength began to fail rapidly.

Once, he fell. Another time he simply sank down in the mud. Both times Jim hoisted him up and gave him a shove.

It was a little past noon when Rumi groped to the edge of a rotten old deadfall-pine, eased down upon the log and muttered something under his breath which Jim did not understand, then he looked around with a glazed stare, and finally stared at Jim.

'I still won't do it,' he mumbled.

Jim did not argue, he stepped over, pulled the Turk away from the dead tree and gave him another of those peremptory shoves. Rumi stumbled ahead.

They came down off a brushy, forested slope to a small creek. Rumi sank down in the grass, pulled off both shoes and plunged his feet into the water. He did not speak, and he did not look around to see where Hewlett was. His entire body sagged. It was as though only his clothing was holding the man together.

Jim sat down, looked over, and said, 'I thought you'd be tougher.'

Rumi was beyond taking offence. 'I ride, I don't walk,' he mumbled. 'When I was a boy, I walked everywhere. Because I *had* to. I made up my mind if I had to, I'd spend my whole life becoming one of the class of people who didn't have to walk. I got up there. I even qualified to be educated in America at state expense.'

'And now you're one of the richest men in the world,' said Jim Hewlett, clasping both hands behind his head and lying back in the grass. 'And you can't even hike twenty miles.'

'You knew it,' accused the Turk. 'You planned it this way. But I'm not going to do it. No matter what you do to me, I'm never going to do it.'

Jim rolled his head a little and studied the man's profile. Hamid Rumi just did not look as though he could be that stubborn or that strong. 'You're going to do it, all right,' he said, with no especial vehemence. 'You're going to do it—or you're going to keep walking until you do. No, I didn't plan it this way, but I'm willing.'

Rumi turned. 'You *did* plan it.'

Jim sighed, still lying back, hands beneath his head. 'Nope. But you can believe whatever you care to—you're going to walk all the way to California—or until you crumble.'

Rumi studied Hewlett, his size, his heft, his torn, ruined suit, and drooped a little more where he sat, allowing the creek water to lower the swelling in his feet.

139

Jim arose, kicked Rumi's shoes closer and said, 'Put them on and let's move out.'

Rumi did not move, for several moments, then he drew his feet out of the water and reached listlessly for his shoes. 'You'll have to go on alone,' he said. 'I can't keep this up without food or rest.'

Jim waited until the Turk had his second shoe on, then reached and with one big hand hoisted the other man to his feet, and shoved him. Rumi turned, teeth bared. Jim smiled. 'Walk!' he said. Rumi continued to glare, then his resolve dwindled, and along with it his will to resist. He had been exposed to rain, to heat, to wind, to mud, and he had been forced to march endless miles without food or rest.

'Half the money,' he muttered. 'I'll give her back half.'

Jim pointed. 'Walk!'

Rumi turned as though to obey, and staggered ahead. He was young enough and sinewy enough to have gone on, but he was far too soft. He halted again and twisted to face Hewlett.

'Half. I said I'd return half the money. Listen to me—'

'Walk!'

Rumi stumbled to a tree and leaned there, looking at Hewlett. 'I don't see how you can do it.' he muttered.

Jim started towards the tree, both large arms rising. Hamid Rumi waved him off. 'Half is more money than she could possibly spend if she lived to be a hundred.'

Jim halted a yard away. 'It's not the damned money, it's how you stole it from her. All of it, or I'm going to stand behind you and kick you the rest of the way to keep you moving.'

Rumi straightened up against the tree. 'You can kill me.'

Jim considered, then said, 'You return every damned penny of it—and—if she's willing to give you *some* of it, a little of it, that'll be up to her. Otherwise . . .' He reached for the thinner man.

Rumi waved him off again. 'All right. All right, I accept the terms. Now for gawd's sake let's find something to eat!'

Chapter Fifteen

Hewlett was of the opinion that unless the authorities had located the stolen whaleboat, they probably only knew that Hamid Rumi had been abducted, without knowing which way his abductor had gone with him.

If they *had* found the whaleboat, had confirmed that two men, one large and thick, one lean and sinewy and dark-headed, had used it, then without much doubt the authorities were searching for Hewlett and his hostage in the state of Washington, and for this reason, when he and Rumi started onward again, Jim's quandary was made especially acute by the fact that all rural villages now had the telephone, and the advent of two strangers, clad in city attire, but ragged and battered and whisker-stubbled, would certainly reach the authorities of some local county, who would pass it on to state and perhaps even federal authorities.

But they still had to eat. Jim was still a long way from being in any personal trouble as a result of his long fast and his exertions. He was a physical-fitness of long standing whose speciality was spartanism. He had undertaken worse treks than this, under even *more* adverse conditions, just to keep in shape. But his immediate problem was not Jim Hewlett, it was Hamid Rumi.

Unless he found a solution to his problem shortly, he was going to have to either abandon his captive, or carry him, and he would not do one, and he could not do the other.

After Rumi's capitulation on the point of full restitution, which was what this entire affair was about, Jim allowed him more frequent stops to rest, and in their shared discomfort, now that there was no longer a block between them, it was possible for them both to achieve some kind of accord.

When they found a narrow road and turned down it, Rumi, whose experience in the uplands and back-country of his native land had fitted him at least for police work in the rural countryside, pointed out that a car, probably a jeep or some similar kind of vehicle, had passed over this narrow road very recently. The tyre-tracks were still quite fresh, in the dry, rain-washed dust. He also said that because the tyres were mud-grips, a variety of tyre commonplace in areas where mud, or even deep dust and sandy-soil were prevalent, and that their tread-pattern was arranged so that traction was aided through *forward* thrust, it was clear that the vehicle had gone outward, past them, perhaps in the direction of some paved, county road.

Jim agreed with this, led the way to the nearest small brushy rise, and down the far side of it, where a small house stood in a grassy clearing, and stood a long while studying this place he intended to burglarise, until Rumi said, 'There are some dogs in a cage out back, but otherwise the place looks empty.'

They went down there, following the road to make a bold frontal approach, trudged to the sagging wooden front porch, and Jim called out. The only answer he got was the baying of hounds round back. He stepped up onto the porch, called again, motioned Rumi up, and together they entered the house by a loose front door.

The house, the yard, and also the interior of the house, were unkempt, slatternly, and none too clean. In the kitchen a rattling old refrigerator yielded half of a roast duck, two bottles of cheap beer, and some chocolate pudding. The cupboard yielded an assortment of tinned fruits and vegetables. Hamid Rumi ate ravenously, and ignored the beer in favour of water from the leaking sink-tap. Jim ate his share, pocketed several tins—and the beer — then fished forth a limp twenty-dollar note and left it atop the makeshift drainboard.

When they left, cutting diagonally across the yard and into the nearest protective thicket of young trees and underbrush, Hamid Rumi pointed to an apple tree with small, rock-hard green apples. Jim shook his head: 'You eat just one of those things and you'll have cramps like you've never had before.'

Rumi's strength returned a little at a time. Eventually, when they halted a mile distant, he lit a limp cigarette with dry matches appropriated back at the cabin, blew smoke, looked all round, then said, 'I've never been in the western United States before. I've always thought of it as either San Francisco or Hollywood. This is like a green jungle.'

Hewlett made no correction, but the heavily timbered northwest was no more like a genuine jungle than Boston was like Los Angeles. The reason he was quiet, was because, now, he had to devise a way to prevent his captive from reneging, once they got back to civilisation. He thought he knew of two ways to prevent this, but he mentioned nothing except their need, finally, to find a large town or a city. He knew that two large cities were not too distant, Tacoma and Seattle, but how they were to be reached, was something else. He decided to turn back in the direction of the shoreline, because in this upper part of the state of Washington, most of the industry, as well as the large cities, were adjacent to the salt-water inlets that cut deeply into the entire north-westerly area.

Hamid Rumi, who had long since lost all sense of direction, trudged along without attempting to converse, his returning strength aided by sustenance, but the bone-tiredness caused by exposure and lack of rest, preventing anything close to total recovery.

They came to a paved throughway, eventually, and in this instance a well-travelled one, the predominant traffic being immense log-carriers. Once, they saw a police cruiser, and Rumi watched it pass from within the fringe of trees where they were standing, with an expression of mixed disgust and cynical acceptance of the fact that, in all lands, when an individual needed the police, they were never available.

They walked parallel to this freeway, prevented from getting any closer to it by a high, chain-link fence, for over a mile. Where there was a turn-off, there was also a break in the steel fencing, but Jim did not go out upon the freeway, he studied the intersecting paved road, and turned eastward. Hamid Rumi scowled, paced along with Jim for a hundred yards, then said, 'This is going to take us back into those damned mountains.'

Jim's answer was curt, but thoughtful. 'This road will take us to a town. What we need now, is a car.'

Rumi didn't pursue this topic, and Hewlett was proven correct when they came up out of a dip in the road and faced a fairly large town dead ahead. Rumi's new mood, after having yielded on the point of the hundred million dollars, was morose and disagreeable. As they walked towards the town he said, 'By now they've found the boat, and maybe the shack where we stole the food.'

'Paid for the food,' corrected Hewlett.

'If they've found out about the food, they'll be spreading the alarm all over this territory. Hewlett, for the last time—fifty thousand dollars, and I'll swear I went with you willingly. They can't prosecute you, then.'

Jim smiled. 'For the last time—you don't have fifty thousand dollars. Remember? You agreed to give it all back to your wife.'

The town was in fact larger than it appeared from the westerly approach. There was probably a large mill somewhere in the area, but also, where the village lay, was a long, somewhat narrow, valley, like an ancient riverbed, between two upthrusts of forested hills, and as far as Jim could see both ways, this valley was under the plough. Farms were visible, with farm-buildings, lush pastures, grazing livestock, and haying equipment. The town itself was alive with cars, pedestrians, even several police cars.

There was a creek beneath a narrow bridge just before Hewlett and Rumi got to the outskirts of town. Jim took Rumi down there with him. They washed, made themselves as presentable as they could, brushed their jackets and put their ties back on. Rumi said, 'All this, just to steal a car?'

Jim did not reply. In fact, he had nothing to say until they had crossed the bridge, then he pointed to a restaurant. 'Hungry?'

The Turk shook his head without speaking,

so Jim took him to the first barber shop, which happened to be empty. It was at the lower end of the town. They were both shorn and shaved and liberally sprinkled with an overwhelmingly sweet-scented after-shave lotion, after the custom of rural American barbers, and when they were back outside in the humid day, Jim said, 'You smell like a Turkish harem.'

Rumi glowered. 'Very funny.' He pointed towards a brick, two-storey buildings mid-way along the busy thoroughfare, where they were standing. 'Police department,' he said, and dropped his arm to stare.

Jim led the way across at an intersection, led the way past the two-storey brick building without a sidewards glance, headed directly towards a travel agency with two signs out front, one above the other, and turned in. Hamid Rumi's expression showed mild bewilderment until Hewlett fished forth his wallet, laid one of those gold-bordered rental-car preference cards upon the counter, and put his Californian driver's licence beside it. The girl behind the counter was impressed by the gold-bordered credit card. She handed Jim a form to sign, ran his credit card through an imprint-machine, and offered Jim a key, along with a dazzling smile, so evidently their somewhat smoothed over disreputable appearance must have been negated by the gold-bordered card.

She even took them round back where the

shiny Fords sat, two rows of them. Jim tipped her with a fiver, and his charming smile, selected a pale blue Ford, climbed in and waited until Rumi was in beside him, then drove out of the parking area, westward, back over the same paved road they had approached the town over, and at the juncture with the freeway, he swung southward. When they were rolling pleasantly along, he smiled at the Turk.

'You're right. Riding is more pleasant than walking.'

Rumi lit a cigarette, loosened his tie, slumped down in the seat, moodily watched the countryside fall rearward for a while, then finally twisted half around so that he was facing Hewlett, and said, 'Maybe the people who live in that shack where we got the food will take your twenty dollar note, and forget it, but that girl back there, has to feed her information through a central clearance system, and *then* the authorities will know where we are.'

'Where we *were*,' stated Hewlett. 'Why don't you just get comfortable and sleep.' Jim turned. 'In the *front* seat.'

Rumi smoked, killed the cigarette after a while, and took a tin of peaches from one jacket pocket, a pilfered opener from the other pocket, opened the can, drank the syrup, and used the opener as an implement to fish out the chunks of fruit and eat them.

149

They saw the spiky cement skyline of a large city dead ahead, and the closer they drove to it, the thicker became the traffic around them. It was rather like being caught up in a wheeled stampede, being carried along in the midst of a motorised herd. Just before they drove over a slight roll in the highway, Jim edged to the left, veered off on a divergency, and from this point on the traffic lessened.

Rumi, finished with his snack, wiped his lips with a soggy handkerchief, watched the road signs for a while, then asked if Jim knew where he was going. Hewlett's answer was good-natured. 'Yeah; to California. But exactly how we get there from here, I haven't the foggiest. Have you?'

Rumi did not answer the question, but he seemed willing to believe Hewlett could do it. 'And after we get there—what?'

'That'll be up to you, Hamid.'

The black eyes came around. 'What do you mean?'

'Well, you see, we've been racking up quite a list of tentative violations. You insisting that you came with me voluntarily, is going to help like hell, of course, but there is still the matter of you being in the US illegally.'

Rumi slowly straightened on the seat. 'Illegally . . . ?'

'Yeah. If I kidnapped you, why then you were forced to sneak across the international border, and the Emigration people will be

150

sympathetic towards you. They'll deport you, send you back to Canada. But if you came voluntarily, Hamid, which means you deliberately sneaked into the country, the Feds are going to get a warrant for your arrest, and be tough.'

'But I didn't come voluntarily!'

Jim turned. 'Didn't you . . . ?'

Rumi fidgeted on the seat. He swore with considerable feeling, because what Jim had left unsaid, but which was suddenly quite apparent, was the fact that unless Hamid Rumi said he came voluntarily, obviously, Hewlett was going to do his utmost to see that Rumi's wife gave him no part of her fortune.

'Blackmail,' said the angry Turk.

Jim did not dispute this. 'But you are alive, which is better than the situation of some people *you've* leaned on. And you can still come out of this smelling roses, depending upon what I recommend to Astarte.'

'Who?'

'Your wife. We call her Astarte.'

Rumi's black eyes bored into Jim Hewlett, who ignored this and concentrated upon his driving.

Chapter Sixteen

They managed to bypass Everett, and Seattle, and were following round the curve of the broken inland shoreline in the direction of Tacoma, when Hewlett said, 'Get some sleep,' to his companion, and the Turk, already on the verge of being overwhelmed by his need of sleep, plus the monotonous gait of their car, obeyed.

Jim, not as physically exhausted as his companion, was not as near collapse, but he was a lot nearer to it than he had allowed the Turk to guess, and driving monotonous mile after monotonous mile did not help one bit.

He changed speeds, hummed to himself, even played the car-radio to ward off the stealing numbness, and in this manner managed to get below the great city of Tacoma, on the road towards Olympia. It was the name of this upcoming city which reminded him of the two bottles of beer he was still carrying. Olympia was where a renowned western beer was manufactured.

He opened one of the bottles and was very careful to sip from it only when there were no cars approaching from the opposite direction. One of the best ways to be stopped by US police was to be seen with an open container in a car.

The beer helped a little, but he had to admit to himself that he was never going to be able to hold out until they reached California. Somewhere along the way, he was going to have to sleep.

Rumi slept through the stop Jim made to tank up with petrol, and even when they entered a mountainous sector where the freeway was not always either level nor straight, the Turk kept right on sleeping. Jim envied him. He also finished his first beer, manoeuvred with his free hand to open a tin of tomatoes, and ate these also, as he drove. Except for the need for rest, he did not feel bad at all.

The day waned, he halted again for petrol, and just ahead of the declining sun, Hamid Rumi awakened, groaned and raised a hand to his neck. Sleeping cramped was less than desirable, but it was, under these circumstances, better by far than not sleeping at all.

He straightened on the seat, looked around, looked at the position of the descending sun, and let go with a loud sigh as he stretched with both arms, pushed hard against the car's floorboards, and turned to look at Hewlett.

Jim smiled. 'Feel better?'

The Turk dropped his hands to his lap, studied Hewlett a long time, then said, 'How in hell do you *do* it?'

Jim laughed. 'Clear conscience.'

Rumi snorted, then said, 'Where are we?'

'Not far from the Oregon line.'

Rumi showed surprise, but he said no more for a while, not until after he'd lighted a cigarette and had studied the rugged countryside, which seemed to impress him less than it troubled him to think that they were actually in a fair way of not being apprehended, after all. Then, a thought came, and he said, 'Do you know why the police aren't making a harder hunt for us?'

Jim shrugged. 'Why?'

'Because they know where we're heading. They know you'll try to get down to Los Angeles with me, and they'll be waiting down there.'

Jim nodded his head gently. 'You're undoubtedly right. But suppose we don't go to Los Angeles?'

Rumi was checked up short by this. 'You're not going to Los Angeles?'

'Do you think, after all I've been through, I'm going to let someone foul me up at the last minute? Hamid, you don't give me much credit.'

Rumi reached to switch on the radio, which Jim had turned off hours back. As the Turk sat hunched, seeking a channel which was broadcasting the news, Jim drove steadily down across a rolling, high hump of rough countryside, and when Rumi finally found a news-channel, coming from Portland, in

Oregon, he turned up the volume and sat listening. Nothing was said of an abduction in Canada, nor the probable flight of a kidnapper and his victim.

Rumi frowned in puzzlement, as Hewlett said, 'Hang in there. Keep trying, there must be one station that'll have the lurid story. Fish around until you locate a Canuck station, maybe in Vancouver, or close by.'

Rumi leaned and twisted the dial. He got music, all kinds of it, ninety-nine per cent bad, and ultimately, when he found another newscast and turned up the volume, the announcer seemed to be reaching as far as he could for things to say, but after fifteen minutes he still had not announced any sensational abduction of a Turkish trade official in Canada, nor his probable route of abduction down across the United States.

Rumi gave the radio a savage twist, lit a cigarette, glared dead ahead out through the windscreen, and said nothing.

They caught sight of the sea, or what Jim thought had to be the sea, shortly after sundown, but the light was too uncertain for them to be certain. They only knew that once again the traffic seemed to be picking up. There were any number of sideroads, all of them spewing forth cars, as though more log-mills back beyond sight from the freeway had just changed shifts, or had ended their daytime operations, at any rate.

They passed a town called Longview. Hamid Rumi leaned to watch for additional signs. The one he finally saw, settled him back as the car breezed swiftly across a state line, then they were in Oregon, and Rumi finished his smoke, put it out very carefully in the dashboard ashtray, and settled back, at long last looking as though he were becoming totally resigned.

'You're going to do it,' he said, wonderingly. 'You're going to bring it off, Hewlett.'

Jim took an inland route, fuelled up for the first time in Oregon, drove through the settling night until he found a dense grove of trees, then, without warning, he pulled over, found an opening, and shot up through some low ferns into a small circular clearing. While Rumi watched, baffled again, Jim climbed from the car, with the keys, stepped round back, opened the boot, saw what he sought, tyre-chains, dragged one out, called to Rumi, and when the rested, revitalised Turk came round back, Jim reached, spun him against the car, lashed the tyre-chain round both Rumi's ankles, then pushed the Turk into a sitting position, aimed a stiff finger at him and said, 'Don't move. Not one damned inch.' Then he pitched the loose end of the chain in front of the rear wheel, got into the car, drove ahead six inches, until the chain was directly beneath the wheel, dead-centre, then Jim climbed out, wordlessly knelt to inspect his work, arose pulled off his jacket and tossed it down. Until he was lying back, Hamid Rumi made no attempt to speak. Then, he did, he said, 'Hewlett, however this thing ends, I would still like you to work for me.'

Jim closed his eyes and relaxed an inch at a time. He said, 'Uh huh.'

'Even without my wife's fortune, I'm not exactly a poor man, Hewlett. I have contacts in London and New York as well as in Berlin and Ankara.'

'Uh, huh.'

'There are great opportunities for men like you, as resourceful as—'

'You son of a bitch,' came the deep voice from the prone man. 'If you don't shut your mouth I'm going to ram a fist down it!'

Hamid Rumi glared, then loosened, then he laughed, and that was the last sound Jim Hewlett heard, until the cold awakened him. Nearby, Hamid Rumi had managed to get all of himself but his feet and ankles into the back seat of their car. He was sound asleep in a grotesque position.

Jim looked at his wrist. It would be dawn shortly, He arose, put on the jacket, swung his arms to stir his sluggish circulation, went over, started the car, backed off the tyre chain, went back to remove the chains from Rumi's ankles, and when he had replaced the chains in the boot, he went over, yanked the Turk awake and said, 'Get up front.'

157

They resumed their drive, and although the rented car lacked a heater, with the windows up the interior became adequately warm after a dozen or so miles.

They encountered very few passenger cars until well after sun-up, but they met any number of those huge log trucks. Rumi made some remark about this, which Jim did not bother replying to.

Rumi asked about the two bottles of beer Jim had brought along, and Jim finally smiled and spoke. 'All gone. I drank it.' He fished in his pockets, brought forth one flat tin of sardines and one round tin of pears. Rumi accepted the pears and went to work opening the tin.

'Do you know that the Turkish government is probably raising hell with the Canadians over my abduction?' he said.

Jim was not very perturbed. 'The Canadians have a long history of talking tough to other nations—which they can afford to do, since they know the US will not allow them to be directly confronted.' He looked at Rumi. 'How many good swimmers do you have in your invasion armies? It's one hell of a long swim from Turkey to Canada.'

'Your humour is awful,' stated the Turk, and offered some of the tinned pears, which Jim declined.

'Never cared for them.'

Rumi looked at the single remaining tin,

158

between them on the seat. 'Do you like sardines?'

'No. But I'll eat them.'

Rumi finished the pears and looked at his clothing. He said he hadn't been this filthy since he'd been a child. Jim passed that off too, with the same comment he'd made before. 'Anything beats being dead.'

Rumi smiled, leaned back, watched the sky brighten, and eventually made another statement. 'Does the private investigation business pay very well, Hewlett?'

Jim answered by excluding his present assignment, which he wouldn't have included in any case, because he never closed a file until an assignment had been completed. 'No, not too well. That is, after four years, I'm just now beginning to score. Why? You thinking of opening an agency in Turkey?'

'I was thinking of working out some kind of partnership with you. Hewlett, you're the damnedest snake-in-the-grass I ever heard of.'

Jim's answer was pensive. 'Thank you—I think. No partnership. Not with you, particularly, and not with anyone else. If I liked being obligated to other people I'd go into banking.'

Rumi took the refusal as though he hadn't expected anything else. 'Suppose my wife has already made up her mind to have me killed. Hewlett, I can tell you something about her: If she *did* decide to have it done, nothing would

159

stop her, and I know for a fact you can hire assassins pretty inexpensively in the US.'

'For a guy who's never been here before, by your own admission, you sure know a lot about us. Or else you're gullible as hell. Anyway, she's not going to do that.'

Rumi looked over. 'How well do you know my wife?'

'I told you. I saw her once. I don't even know her name.'

'Then you have no idea what she's capable of.'

'Hamid, if she tried to get you hit, I wouldn't blame her one damned bit, and if you'd stuck that knife into my back, and tossed me overboard, I'd have killed you back in the hotel room in Canada . . . But she's *still* not going to have you killed.'

'You guarantee it, Hewlett?'

'Yeah, Hamid, I guarantee it.'

They drove through the rising sunlight across a countryside which was largely mountainous, but seemed to have chains of fertile valleys between almost every upthrust. Oregon looked to Jim Hewlett like a haven for small farmers. Every way he looked, there were farms, and none of them seemed to be either very large, or arid. It was, he thought, an ideal place for people to retire to, who liked living in the boondocks. His personal preferences did not incline in that direction.

Evidently Hamid Rumi had some similar

160

kind of thoughts, because, as they skirted round a large metropolitan area called Salem, Rumi said, 'Agriculture seems to be the main business in this place.' Then, speaking more thoughtfully, he made an observation a Turk in Oregon for the first time was bound to make, sooner or later. 'Water. It must rain here every week or two, as it does in the New England states . . . Hewlett, if we had this much irrigation in my country, in the parts where they now grow opium, you Americans wouldn't have to bribe the peasants not to plant poppies.' He turned, half smiling in a mocking manner. 'Why don't you suggest to your give-away damned fools in Washington that what they *should* do, instead of trying to buy us off, which will fail, of course, is put that same money into developing water for our farmers?'

'Sure,' Jim answered. 'I'll take it up with the President the next time he calls me. Now why don't you shut up for a while?'

Chapter Seventeen

Oregon was a green and picturesque state to drive the full length of, but after a while it became monotonously the same. The last time they stopped for fuel Hamid Rumi bought a packet of cigarettes, and Jim bought a large bag of fruit, then they resumed their tiresome trip, right on down through the mountains of southern Oregon, keeping abreast of the darkness.

They had no idea when they finally passed over into California, although there surely was a sign to signify this un-momentous event, and they had the good fortune to pass through the countryside just below the California-Oregon border in darkness, for although the country was majestically rugged—and poor—the few settlements were functionally ugly and depressingly coarse and common.

They had to cover four hundred miles before reaching San Francisco, and this was accomplished so that they shot across the Golden Gate Bridge ahead of the inundating swarm of early-morning traffic, just ahead of sunrise.

Rumi slept until Jim jabbed him awake at the bridge, then Rumi straightened up to look around. He did not say whether he was impressed or not, but he yawned on the far side, dug two purple plums from the bag of fruit and ate them for breakfast.

Jim explained where they were. Rumi acknowledged all the things Hewlett told him, then, while running a set of bent fingers through his curly black hair, he said, 'I'd give a hundred dollars for a bath.'

Hewlett nodded sympathetically. 'Be patient. That's exactly what I've got in mind for both of us.'

He said no more, and although Rumi looked at him, a little perplexed, he did not pursue this topic with any questions.

Jim re-fuelled for the last time, angled from the inland highway to the coast highway, which was spectacularly breathtaking in places, with a superb view—and also with a very unsettling sheer drop to the rocks below on the beaches —and finally began to relax, something which was reflected in his driving. He slackened speed.

They were near the town of Santa Maria when Jim found an isolated telephone kiosk at roadside, took the keys of the car with him, and while putting in a call to Mary Friday, faced the car. But Rumi ignored both Hewlett and the opportunity for leaping from the car and running. He fished in the bag of fruit, came up with a peach this time, and sat in rumpled relaxation while he ate it.

When Mary Friday heard Jim Hewlett's

voice she made a small, but audible gasp. 'Where *are* you? Benedict and Fleisher have called at least three times a day since.'

'*Who* called, Hollingsworth?'

'Yes. He came round last evening too. But this morning it was Mr Benedict himself. They're very upset.'

Jim's reply was dry. 'I can imagine.' Then he said, 'Friday, I want you to call Mr Benedict. *Not* Hollingsworth. Mr Benedict. You understand?'

'Yes. I'm only to speak to Mr Benedict.'

'You're wonderful. And tell him I want to see *him,* no one else, and least of all Carl Hollingsworth, *with* Astarte. I want to see them at precisely four o'clock this afternoon—on my boat in Santa Monica Harbour. And Friday—don't call from the office, go downstairs and call from a pay-phone. No one but Mr Benedict is to know I'm at the boat. Impress upon him that if he tells anyone, he's not only going to lose his only chance for recovering Astarte's fortune for her, but he's also going to be up to his butt in trouble with the FBI, because they'd give a lot, right about now, to find me.'

'I'll do exactly as you say, Mr Hewlett.'

Jim smiled out the opened kiosk door in the direction of the disinterested, peach-eating Turk. 'That's the kind of an answer a man likes to hear from a woman. You'll make someone a hell of a good wife, Friday.'

164

She came right back. 'Interested. Mr Hewlett?'

He side-stepped a commitment. 'There is something I haven't figured out yet, lover: There is absolutely nothing on the radio about a prominent Turkish trade commissioner being abducted in Canada. That should have hit the headlines like thunder out of China.'

'If you wish, I'll call one of the radio stations and enquire.

'No, forget it. Just do the other things, and you'll help a lot. Be sure and impress on Mr Benedict that no one is to know I'm on the boat.'

'Yes.'

'Good-bye.' He hung up the receiver, stepped out of the kiosk, and as he approached the car one of California's black-and-white Highway Patrol cars cruised past, its driver not even looking to his left.

Rumi was wiping peach-juice off his hands as they resumed their drive. He looked enquiringly up, once, and said, 'You've lined up your private army?'

Jim smiled. 'An army of one man.'

Rumi kept looking at Hewlett. 'Do you remember what you said about guaranteeing that my wife won't have me—?'

'Listen, Hamid, if anyone tries to have you hit, it won't be Astarte, because she doesn't know where you are, but it *could* be someone else.'

'Who?'

'Hollingsworth, of Benedict and Fleisher,' stated Hewlett. 'A man who will sell out once, will do it again, and this particular bastard has certainly been comparing the bribe you sent down to him, with the total amount of the money being tossed around in this affair. He's had a week or so to start thinking in terms of millions, instead of thousands.'

'How would killing me help him?'

'Your wife would inherit—or should I have said *re*-inherit? She is *here* in California, and so is Hollingsworth, and you've already established a precedent by trying to kill her for her fortune.'

Rumi's low, broad forehead crinkled. 'Hollingsworth is that capable?'

Jim shrugged. 'How would I know? He sold me out to you, didn't he? It's just a guess on my part, but Hollingsworth *did* know I went north to hunt you down. Maybe, this time, he's sold me out to the FBI or the police—and maybe he's laying a little murder-trap of his own.'

'Then what in the hell are you thinking of, coming down here, getting this close to him?' Rumi demanded.

Jim yawned, stretched one arm at a time, ignored the Turk's question, and when he finally reached a safe stretch of roadway, he made a long study of the sea and surf on their right. Despite all that was said in favour of

California, its views, its climate, its fertility, and its magnificent surf and beaches, the Pacific Ocean was not always a friendly sea.

But today it was. By the time Hewlett and the Turk were passing through the environs of Santa Barbara, they saw a number of small craft a mile or two beyond the surf, many of them under sail, and farther out, like white specks upon an eternity of slatey-green, were the larger and more venturesome craft, not all pleasure-craft. Some rode low enough in the water to suggest that commercial fishing was productive, even this close to the shore.

It was mid-afternoon when they came down the Coast Highway, with Santa Monica and the lower headlands in sight. Rumi's interest was stronger here, and when Jim unexpectedly swung off the highway and threaded his way through narrower, older roadways, reaching a sea-front parking lot full of other cars, the Turk's interest became noticeably greater.

As Jim left the car he said, 'Bring along whatever's left of the fruit—and that can of sardines.'

Rumi obeyed. They trooped down the slightly sloping terrain, crossed two hectically-busy commercial avenues, reached the vicinity of the man-made breakwater of huge stones, and finally left all pavement behind and walked in sand to the dinghy. Only when they were in the little ship-to-shore boat, with Jim at the oars, did Hamid Rumi say, 'Of course. I should have guessed it would be something like this, back up in the whaleboat. Only after we'd landed, up there, did it occur to me that you weren't the terrible seaman I'd thought. You seemed to be, on purpose. Now this.'

Jim laughed. 'You're smart enough, Hamid. Just slow.' He rowed to the sparkling, immaculate, combination motor-and-sail craft riding lazily at anchor, secured the dinghy and went aboard first, then beckoned the Turk aboard. Jim gestured widely. 'You can stretch, sleep, eat, anything you care to do. And since I promised you a bath.' He pointed. 'Dive in.'

Rumi stepped into the shade of the aft canopy and gazed around where dozens of other craft, many smaller, some larger, also rode at anchor behind the protective bulwark of another vast stone seawall, between the harbour and the open sea. As he turned back, he lit a cigarette, flipped the match into the water, and said, 'How long?'

Jim looked at his wrist watch. 'No more than an hour.'

'Then what, Hewlett?'

'That's pretty much up to you, Hamid.' Jim smiled. 'And the next time you call me *Hewlett,* I'm going to break one of your arms. And the time after that, another one of your arms. And the time after that, an ankle. And—'

'All right, all right.' Hamid Rumi sighed, glanced round at the boat, lifted his black eyes again, and made a crooked smile. 'You're

168

going to win. *Mr* Hewlett, without more than the barest damned chance, when you first appeared in that hotel doorway, you've managed to bring it off.'

Jim removed his jacket and flung it behind him, down into the cabin. Then his tie, his shirt, and his shoes. Finally, as he shed his trousers, he gestured for the Turk to do the same. 'You can swim, can't you?'

Instead of replying right away, Hamid Rumi also began to strip. Jim stopped him, finally. 'Keep your shorts on. They're a little old-fashioned in the harbour.' He beckoned. 'Dive in.'

Rumi did. He was an excellent swimmer, but when Jim surfaced nearby and waggled a finger in warning, Rumi said, 'I'm not going to try and swim for it. I'm too interested, by now.'

They swam for a half hour, climbed back aboard the boat, and Jim broke out two bottles of beer. They lay in hot shade beneath the stern canopy, drying off. When Jim went below for the second brace of beers, the Turk rolled onto his back, stretched out full length, and when Jim handed him the glass he said, 'Thanks. This has been quite an experience. I think if my wife had gone to Marseilles or Liverpool, or perhaps to Greece, instead of to California, I'd be dead by now.'

'If you thought that, why did you try and beat her out of the money in the first place?' Jim asked.

Rumi laughed. 'What's a life in comparison to a hundred million dollars? Even my own life. Incidentally, those men with me, up in Vancouver, they weren't trade commissioners, they were bodyguards.'

Jim sank back upon the circular, upholstered bench of the stern-well, half smiling. 'Next time, just change your identity— become a woman—and lose yourself in Paris or New York. If those guys weren't trade commissioners . . . what then?'

Rumi continued to gaze comfortably up at the protective canvas canopy as he answered. 'I *bought* that designation; for fifty thousand dollars a very high official of the Turkish government fixed us up with trade-commissioners credentials. We had to act the part, for the benefit of the Canadians, otherwise they wouldn't have extended us an official welcome—complete with a regiment of police for protection.' Rumi turned his sophisticated, dark gaze to Jim Hewlett. 'Do you know any safer way to arrive in a foreign country with more than ninety million dollars worth of negotiable bonds?'

Jim didn't. 'No. What did you do with them?'

'Deposited eighty million in a bank up there, to be cashed out, and the money to be held for me until I decided upon an investment dispersion programme. About ten million to be negotiated, converted to cash, and held in a private account subject to my withdrawal as expense-money.' Rumi sat up, drained his second glass of beer, and watched a small boat push off from the far shoreline as he said, 'I'll tell you something, Jim Hewlett,' he slowly turned his face towards Jim. 'It's impossible to think in terms of tens of millions. Maybe that's just me, but when those bankers started telling me of the investment opportunities in Canada, talking in terms of ten and twenty millions, or even five millions, I couldn't actually envision that amount of money, nor all the buildings and machinery and trucking facilities, and offices and people, and markets, I would be getting for that money.' He grinned and shook his head.

Jim said, 'Another beer?'

Rumi turned back to watching the distant dinghy. 'No. Maybe after my wife and that man with her have departed, but for what I see ahead for me, I think I'd better have a perfectly clear head.'

Jim turned, also studied the approaching dinghy, and committed a crime against Mother Nature and all the nattering brainless environmentalists by dropping his empty beer bottle over the side.

Chapter Eighteen

The two men on the boat watched the beautiful woman and hardly more than glanced at the slightly hawk-faced, grey-headed, tanned, fit man who had rowed her out. David Benedict could have been simply a hired oarsman for all the attention he received as Jim Hewlett stepped ahead and lent a hand to the beautiful woman who stepped aboard, first. Benedict came aboard last, secured the dinghy, and turned to put a slow, assessing stare upon Hamid Rumi. But Rumi's wife, although she stared in a totally expressionless way at her husband, until she was aboard, afterwards moved over in front of Jim Hewlett with her very dark eyes lifted in frank concern, and said, 'Are you all right?'

Jim smiled into the lifted, beautiful face. 'I'm fine.'

Mr Benedict crossed over looking harrassed and hostile. 'Why in the name of heaven did you abduct him and bring him all the way back down here, Hewlett?'

Jim's smile lingered as he replied. 'I didn't abduct him, Mr Benedict, he came voluntarily.'

Benedict turned abruptly, scowling at the Turk, then he swung back to Jim again. 'In case you are interested, Hewlett, that man's passport is still lying on a dresser at the

Dunhill hotel, up in Vancouver.'

Jim continued to smile. 'All right. He's in the country illegally. They can deport him. But not just yet.' Jim leaned and tapped the older man's chest with a large, stiff finger. 'And that son of a bitch who works for you, Hollingsworth, sold you and Astarte, and me, to Mr Rumi, for fifteen thousand dollars, cash. Rumi knew I was up there looking for him. I damned near didn't make the contact. Mr Benedict, if Hollingsworth is still in the city next week, I'm going to break his neck. That's a promise.'

Benedict turned towards Hamid Rumi, who was slouching upon the circular seat at the stern of the boat, amused. He nodded at Mr Benedict's glare. 'That's right, solicitor, Hollingsworth sold the lot of you out to me, for cash. But this damned fool persisted. I can't begin to explain how he pulled it off, but here I am—illegally, of course.'

Jim said, 'Voluntarily, Hamid.' and the amused Turk nodded, avoiding his wife's eyes. 'Voluntarily, Mr Benedict.'

Astarte, still standing very close to Jim, slowly swung about and stared icily at the man who had tried to murder her. 'I am going to have you killed,' she said, very softly, and the amused look slowly vanished from Rumi's face, but instead of retorting, instead of speaking at all, he looked past the beautiful woman, past the lawyer, straight at Jim

Hewlett.

Jim tapped Astarte's shoulder. 'He will re-assign your fortune to you. It's in a Canadian bank.' Jim raised his eyes to Hamid Rumi. 'Most of it's in a Canadian bank. He told me he'd deposited negotiable securities to the tune of eighty million, and another ten millions worth to be cashed and held for his use. That leaves ten million unaccounted for.'

Rumi's black eyes remained upon Jim's face. 'Half to you,' he said, casually, 'and half to me.'

David Benedict broke in. '*All* of it, Mr Rumi. Every blasted penny of it.'

The black eyes flickered to Benedict. 'You heard her, didn't you. She's going to have me killed. Under these conditions, Mr Benedict, I'll keep the ten million. What will I lose?'

Jim interrupted. 'She's *not* going to hire someone to kill you.'

Rumi's black brows rose a notch. 'That's your guarantee, again?'

'Yes,' stated Jim, and tapped the beautiful woman's arm again. 'That's the price of his voluntary accompaniment back here with me.'

David Benedict sputtered. 'My gawd, Hewlett—*ten million dollars*?'

Jim's answer was curt. 'Ten per cent is the usual finder's fee, isn't it, Mr Benedict?'

'But you agreed to accept—'

'Sure I did, and I'll stick to the signed agreement. The ten million isn't *mine*, it's *his*.'

174

Jim looked at Rumi, 'I told you, I wouldn't work for you. That includes taking half the ten million.' He smiled. 'She isn't going to give you that much anyway.'

The black eyes bored into Jim. 'No . . . ?'

'No. She'll give you one million.'

Astarte stiffened, and turned, glaring from one of them to the other. '*I* say what's to be done here, not either one of you.'

Hamid Rumi's eyes crinkled into a tough, sardonic smile. 'Jim; *now* does it make sense to you, why I tried to kill her?'

Hewlett's answer was cold. 'No. You don't kill everyone you don't like, not even in Turkey.' He looked downward. 'Astarte, give him the million.'

'Never. I'll give it to *you,* if you'll kill him.'

'No one's going to kill anyone,' stated Jim. 'Damn it all.' He turned on David Benedict. 'Can you arrange to have the fortune returned to her, legally?'

'Yes, of course,' replied the barrister. 'That's what I was hired to accomplish. In fact, after I talked to your girl this morning, I had the papers brought in and I've got them in my pocket.' Benedict turned on the beautiful woman. 'And madam, Benedict and Fleisher will have nothing to do with murder.'

Astarte's colour mounted. She looked steadily at David Benedict for a long moment, until Jim Hewlett reached, took her by the arm, swung her half around and shoved her down the narrow stairway leading to the below-decks cabin. Then Jim pointed a finger at Hamid and said, 'You'd better be here when I return.'

Hamid laughed. 'I wouldn't leave now, old boy.'

David Benedict, scowling and uncertain, glared at Hewlett as though he would say something, but Jim turned the same pointing finger on the prestigious barrister, and waggled it. He did not say a word, then he turned and went down the narrow ladder into the cabin, closed the door, and turned to find Astarte standing over by the galley sink, her back to the woodwork, holding her purse in both hands.

He did not move towards her. Once before, she had stood like this, and he had thought she was probably the most beautiful woman he'd ever known, that other time. This time, he still thought she was, so he simply said, 'Don't destroy my image of you.'

Her anger flashed out at him. 'My image to you! Do you realise what that man out there tried to do to me!'

'But he didn't succeed, did he?'

'In my country we repay treachery *with*—'

'Damn it, Astarte, you're not *in* your country.'

She glared. 'You want him to go free, after all he did?'

'No. But I'm not going to kill him, and

you're not going to have him killed, either.'

'Jim, he's a professional assassin. He represents the opium interests.'

Hewlett rolled up his eyes. 'Lady, it seems to me as though everyone in your country is up to their necks in some aspect of the opium traffic. As for his being an assassin—he's never killed anyone in the US. The rest of it's the business of the Turkish government.'

'He's charmed you,' she exclaimed.

Jim laughed. 'There is only one Turk in this wide world who has ever charmed me—who ever *could* charm me—and believe me, Hamid Rumi sure as hell isn't . . . . He shoved off the door and crossed over to her. She seemed to want to push back, to get farther away from him, but it was a very small cabin.

He reached, took the purse from her, started to fling it upon the bunk nearby, then hesitated, hefting it, and finally he pulled the draw-strings, opened the purse, lifted out the pearl-handled automatic pistol, and *then* tossed the purse on the bunk as he sardonically gazed at her.

'What in the hell were you going to do with this thing?' he asked, and gave her no chance to answer as he stepped to a porthole and flung the gun out into the sea. 'Listen, Astarte, I don't like to reward attempted murder and embezzlement any better than you do, but I abducted your husband, crossed an international border with him, and kept him a prisoner until I could deliver him, down here. That happened to be the only really certain way I could think of, to make damned certain he transferred the fortune back to you. If I'd forced him to sign a quit-claim up in Canada, he'd have repudiated it before I'd got back across the damned border. Do you understand this part of it? And if I'd brought him down here against his will, the FBI and probably the Canadian police, and just about anyone you can think of who doesn't like abduction, would be swarming all over the place looking for me. So—I brought him here to make damned certain you got your money back. It was the only dependable way to accomplish that . . . Astarte, the cost is one million dollars, to him. Now, damn it all, that leaves you ninety-nine millions. Is that so terrible?'

She stood looking up, all the while he was talking. When he finished, she loosened a little, and shifted her glance briefly, as she replied. 'No. But I should hire someone to—'

'Stop talking like that, will you!' He grabbed her by the upper arms. It acted like a trigger on them both. She slid her arms round his middle, low, and pulled herself against him, full length. She tipped her face just as his head and shoulders bent downwards. The kiss was tender, at first, then savage and demanding, and when he pushed clear, she held his eyes with her blazing black gaze and said, '*That* was the one million dollar kiss.' Then she released him, raised a hand to push back her hair, and said, 'Let him go back with Mr Benedict. Let him go anywhere, just as long as he gets off this boat, gets out of my sight.' She raised a hand to his chest, and pushed. 'Go up there and get rid of them both. I'll stay here.'

He straightened back. For a moment they stood there, looking at one another, then she very slowly smiled. 'Please . . . ?'

He turned and crossed the little cabin, stepped up onto the deck, and saw the look in the black eyes of the Turk, the *knowing* look. He said, 'Mr Benedict, it's your baby from this point on. Take him to your office, anywhere you want to take him, and have the papers legally signed.'

David Benedict flicked a glance in the direction of the empty few stairs behind Jim, as though expecting to see Astarte back there. The stairs remained empty. Benedict sighed. 'He gets the one million?'

Jim nodded, shifting his glance to the Turk. 'He gets the one million . . . Hamid?'

Rumi lifted bare shoulders. 'You've said it over and over, haven't you? I'm alive, aren't I? And I saw what that was you tossed out the porthole. I saw it, pearl-handles and all, before it hit the water.'

Jim turned back to the attorney. 'You're also to do what you can to get Rumi out of the country without the Emigration people making trouble.'

179

David Benedict's eyes widened. 'How?'

Jim had no idea. 'You're the lawyer, I'm not. You'll think of something. It's a fat fee, you're getting, isn't it?'

David Benedict turned to Hamid Rumi, and pointed towards the dinghy. The Turk stepped over the side into the small craft, and as Benedict leaned to untie the line, Rumi called up to Hewlett. 'Come to Ankara some time, *Mr* Hewlett.' He smiled. 'It's still hard to believe that you brought it off.'

As Mr Benedict straightened up, line in hand, he said, 'For a hundred thousand dollars, I expected success.'

Hamid Rumi stared. 'A hundred thousand? Jim, you damned fool, I offered you fifty times . . .' He checked himself, steadied the boat until the lawyer was safely on his seat amidships, then Rumi simply stared at Hewlett, shaking his head. David Benedict unshipped the oars, set his back to the larger vessel, and rowed with long, experienced sweeps.

Jim watched them depart. Astarte came up onto deck, looked, then said, 'He's going into the city like that—without his clothes on?'

Jim hadn't thought of that. They were too distant to hear his shout. He turned to her. 'Mr Benedict will think of something.'

She laughed up into his face. He smiled down at her. 'Now it's different, Astarte. Before, you were a destitute, very beautiful

180

woman. Now—well hell—you've got to be one of the richest women in the world. I'm self-conscious around you.'

She flung her arms wide. 'But I'm still a destitute woman. They haven't even reached Mr Benedict's car yet. They won't get back to his office to sign the papers for another hour.' She dropped her arms, gazed round, then said. 'I *still* don't have a bathing suit,' and slowly raised black eyes to his face. 'Is there a law . . . After sundown, when they can't see us from the shore, is there a law against us swimming in the—moonlight?'

He was sure there *was* a law, but this one would be the *least* law he'd broken in the past several days, when he hadn't done anything *but* break laws.

He took her down into the cabin to prepare a light meal. He was starved.

We hope you have enjoyed this Large Print book. Other Chivers Press or Thorndike Press Large Print books are available at your library or directly from the publishers.

For more information about current and forthcoming titles, please call or write, without obligation, to:

Chivers Large Print
published by BBC Audiobooks Ltd
St James House, The Square
Lower Bristol Road
Bath BA2 3BH
UK
email: bbcaudiobooks@bbc.co.uk
www.bbcaudiobooks.co.uk

OR

Thorndike Press
295 Kennedy Memorial Drive
Waterville
Maine 04901
USA
www.gale.com/thorndike
www.gale.com/wheeler

All our Large Print titles are designed for easy reading, and all our books are made to last.